THE PRISONER

HANK STINE was a *nom de guerre* of Jean Marie Stine, author of *Double Your Brain Power, Writing Successful Self-Help & How-To Books,* and co-author of *Best Guide to Meditation.* She has also written under the *nom de plumes* Allan Jorgenson and Sibly Whyte. Her erotic science fiction novel, *Season of the Witch* (1968) was reprinted in 1995 when the non-erotic movie version, *Synapse* (*Memory Run* in Europe), was filmed. In addition to writing *Season of the Witch*, Jean Marie Stine has served on the Board of Directors of the International Foundation for Gender Education and the Gay, Lesbian, Bisexual, and Transgender Political Alliance of Western Massachusetts. She has written extensively for both science fiction and transgender publications, including *Amazing Stories, Transformation, Galaxy,* and *Transgender Tapestry.*

AVAILABLE NOW

THE PRISONER COLLECTION

The Prisoner
by Thomas Disch

The Prisoner: A Day in the Life
by Hank Stine

*The Prisoner: The Official Companion
to the Classic TV Series*
by Robert Fairclough

THE PRISONER
A DAY IN THE LIFE

HANK STINE

ibooks

new york
www.ibooks.net
DISTRIBUTED BY SIMON & SCHUSTER, INC.

A Publication of ibooks, inc.

The Prisoner™ and © 1967 and 2001
Carlton International Media Limited.
Licensed by Carlton International Media Limited.
Represented by Bliss House, Inc.,
West Springfield, MA 01089-4107

An ibooks, inc. Book

All rights reserved, including the right to reproduce this book
or portions thereof in any form whatsoever.
Distributed by Simon & Schuster, Inc.
1230 Avenue of the Americas, New York, NY 10020

ibooks, inc.
24 West 25th Street
New York, NY 10010

The ibooks World Wide Web Site Address is:
http://www.ibooks.net

ISBN 0-7434-5275-5
First ibooks, inc. printing December 2003
10 9 8 7 6 5 4 3 2 1

Cover photograph
copyright © 2002 by Carlton International

Printed in the U.S.A.

For the old reality freaks:
Hedberg, Sandy and Pippin;
And some new ones:
Rudolph, Goldsmith and Karen.

Music pounds out of the car's speaker with a steady insistent rhythm and the singer's voice sets up an eerie summons, high and compelling. It is a rock song, *White Rabbit*. Hard as daylight, the song wails on—the shadows of overhead trees dappling and swirling off the car as it roars down the highway and into the city.

The driver's face is grim and set. Eyes, chin, plane of the face, tightness of mouth, determined, stubborn and intractable. A dark blue scarf blows back from the throat of his jacket and his eyes stare intently ahead. The woman's image is conjured in the darkness of his mind, behind the brightness of London, its flat greens and sooty stone.

The car moves smoothly through the traffic, passing, turning and accelerating with a swift, sure expertise. The man's face is set unswervingly into the pounding uncertainty of the music. His eyes glitter and he smiles grimly, taking out a cigar and bringing it to his lips. Music and city blend into one kaleidoscopic rhythm: concrete and drums.

The music reaches an eerie, wailing climax, and the car drops down a ramp into an underground garage.

He gets out of the car and goes up to giant, double doors, throwing them open with a defiant downward jerk of his arms. He comes to a desk, glares at its occupant, whips an envelope from his pocket, slams it on the blotter, turns, exits.

A card goes up from a computer. Typewriter keys slam against it. The man's photograph is xxx'ed out.

The card passes down a conveyor, drops in a file. The file shuts. Its legend moves into the light: RESIGNED.

THE PRISONER

The man's car roars back through the traffic. His eyes gleam and there is a ruthless tilt to his jaw. A hearse is parked at the kerb before his house.

He gets out and goes in. Two men in black high silk hats, with black kerchiefs at the neck, look up after him.

He throws a group of travel folders in an already packed valise and begins to close it. A white fog swirls up about him. He turns and looks. A jet of gas comes in through the keyhole.

He straightens: the room spins.

The spire of St Paul's, seen through the window, spirals in against him. As he falls, his arm knocks the valise to the floor. Clothes and folders spill upon the carpet.

One of the folders falls flat beside his face. A name is printed beneath white gingerbread houses with grey-gabled roofs: PENRHYNDEUDRAETH: PORTMEIRION.

One

Some mornings it was:
'*Guten Morgen, Nummer Sechs.*' Number 105 straightened from her rose bushes and fluttered roughened, pudgy fingers at him.

'*Wie geht es Ihnen?*'

This interest seemed to please her, and she smiled, tucking a straying grey hair back beneath her scarf. '*Gut, danke, und Ihnen?*'

'*Gut, danke.*'

Beyond her yard, the street widened, winding down along the green, past the grocer's, to the sea.

Ting-a-ling-ling.

The bell above the door rang sharply in the dim, musky interior.

Number 87 looked up from the morning paper. 'Ah, it's you, Number Six.' His fat cheeks bowed in a smile. 'I've been expecting you. That order of pickled herring just came in.'

'I'd also like a half-dozen eggs, a five pound bag of flour, and some especially sharp cheddar.'

'Cheddar?' Number 87 scratched dubiously behind his ear. 'Oh, yes. Just the thing for you.' He lifted the flap of the counter and came out around it, going to a group of wooden barrels in the shadow of one wall. He pushed back a cloth cover and produced a bit of rich golden cheese. 'Try this.'

'Satisfactory. Quite satisfactory.'

'I thought you'd like it.' Number 87 nodded and smiled. 'How much?'

'A half-pound, I should think.'

'Want to make it a whole pound, just to be sure?'

'No. Definitely a half.'

THE PRISONER

'Right-o, Number Six.' He busied himself weighing cheese, counting eggs, and getting the flour from its shelf. 'Anything else for you today?' he said, doing the sum on a length of butcher's paper.

'Not today.'

'That will be one point one five credit units.'

'Charge it to my account.'

'Good enough.'

'And could you deliver this afternoon, about five?'

'Right-o.' He rolled it all together in the paper and tied the bundle with a string. 'I'll have Number Twenty-four bring it round. That is, if he ever gets here.' Number 87 frowned, though his eyes remained merry and active. 'Not dependable, you know. That's the way with youngsters these days. Not dependable.' He shook his head in emphasis.

'Be seeing you.'

Number 87 sketched a salute. 'Be seeing you, Number Six.'

Ting-a-ling-ling.

There was music playing on the speakers outside, and as the sun brightened, warming, people began to appear on the green and in the windy, gravelled lanes between the houses.

'Good day, Number Six.' Number 237 appeared from a side street, sweeping off his battered fisher's hat and waving. Then he hurried and caught up. 'Where are you off to today?'

'A chess game with the Admiral.'

'Is that right? Never learned myself, you know.' His scrubbed, honest face furrowed. 'Not my sort of thing. More a hunting and fishing man, myself. Like to watch wrestling on TV. That sort of thing.'

He was silent for a moment.

A DAY IN THE LIFE

'You know something, Number Six?'

'What?'

'They're having a chess tournament in Village Hall next month, you really ought to enter.'

'Why?'

'It'd be fun. I enter the fishing contest, myself. Won two years running. Not last year though. That was Number Eighty-seven. His first time, too. Going down to sign up now. Want to come with me and enter the chess tournament?'

'No thank you, Two Thirty-seven.'

'Well, this is where I turn off. Some other time, maybe.'

His hand swung in a hearty backslap, 'Be seeing you,' and he was off along the lane towards the Civic Centre.

Ting-a-ling-ling. The bell above the door rang. Inside it was cool, dark, sweet with the scent of tobacco.

'*Bonjour*, Number Six. How are you today?' The leathery old man continued rolling a cigar.

'Well enough, thank you, One Fifty-seven. And you?'

'Pretty well myself.' He set the cigar aside to dry.

'You'll be wanting your specials, right?'

'Two dozen.'

'Just a moment.' He got up and went through a curtain to the back.

Ting-a-ling-ling.

'Number One Fifty—' The woman stopped. 'Oh! Hello, Number Six.' Her flowered dress swung against too full a figure. 'I didn't see you here.' She looked around. 'Where's One Fifty-seven?'

'In the—'

'Here I am.'

'There you are.'

Number 157 placed a box on the counter. 'Shall I wrap it?'

THE PRISONER

'No. I'll take it.'
'There's the strangest thing going on outside.'
'Here you are.'
'Thank you.'
'They're making some kind of film.'
'I'll have to put in a new order soon.'
'Please do—'
'Do you know anything about it, Number Six?'
'—and put this on my account. No, I don't, Number Thirty-two.'

Her look was speculative and inviting.

'That's too bad, Number Six. How about you, One Fifty-seven?'

'What's this about a film?'

'There.' She pointed through the window. Four young men stood around a camera, and a fifth stood behind it, eye to the lens, face hidden, looking through it towards the shop.

'*Qu'est-ce que c'est que ceci?* What are they doing to my store?'

Ting-a-ling-ling.

One of the youths came through the door, stuffing a handkerchief into the hip pocket of his denim slacks. 'Hiya, pops. My mates and me'—he indicated the others around the camera—'are doing our term project in Filmmaking. You remember, the course was announced last spring. And we were wondering if you wouldn't mind if we took some shots of you at work?'

'Me? Working? *Je ne compre*—I mean: Why?'

The youth shoved his hands into the pockets of his black leather jacket. 'Well, it's a kind of documentary. There's so much to do and see here, so many interesting people and events, that we...my mates and me...we thought we'd try to show the old and the new. What it has been like and what it will be like.'

'Oh. *Oui*. Whatever you like.'

'And you, sir,' the youth smiled: blond and engaging. 'I didn't catch your number.'

'Don't you know?' Number 32 said. 'This is Number Six.'

'Gosh, is that right, sir. I've heard a lot about you.'

'Have you?'

'Oh, yes. A great deal. They think highly of you in this Village.'

'Do they?'

'Yes. Me mother talks about you sometimes. And me mate, Number Twenty-four. He says you're a regular sort. Would you like to be in our film? I'm sure everyone would like to see you. You're not out much, I hear.'

'No, thank you. I'm already late for an appointment.'

'Say, that's too bad. Some other time?'

'Perhaps. Good day—'

'Number Five Sixty-nine.'

'And to you, too, Number Thirty-two.'

'Where are you going?'

'To chess with the Admiral.'

'The Admiral. Say, I'll bet he'd be a good subject for our film. He's been here longer than anybody.'

'*A bientôt*, Number Six.'

'Be seeing you, One fifty-seven.'

'Say, Miss—'

'Thirty-two. But it's Mrs. really. My husband died.'

'That's too bad.'

'Oh, it was some time ago.'

'Well, would you care to—'

Ting-a-ling-ling.

A sharp, cool breeze had sprung up from the sea,

smelling of salt water in the sleepy afternoon sunshine. The group around the camera glanced up curiously, then turned back to their conversation.

Down the beach (past the deck chairs with their red and white striped umbrellas) the Village Restaurant was just opening. Number One Twenty-seven was busying herself about the patio tables, whisking off the night's residue of grit and moisture, and preparing for the day's clientele. She stopped for a moment and waved: the fragile face beneath her tarnished blonde hair showing no trace of the bitterness that had led her to attempt suicide in the water so near at hand.

'Ah, Number Six. Been wondering when you'd get here.' The Admiral displayed the open board, figures ranked upon it.

'Good day, Admiral. Sorry to be late.'

'Think nothing of it. Happened to be late myself. A touch of stiffness in my bones this morning.'

'Nothing serious, I trust.'

'Damme, lad, only an old man's aches and pains. Don't give it a second thought.' His huge gentle fingers opened to reveal two pawns: one black, one white. He hid them behind his back, then held out both hands, palms closed. 'Choose.'

'That one.'

The right contained: black.

They made the traditional opening: Queen's pawns to Queen's four.

The new girl came out, wearing a terrycloth robe over her swim suit, and moved one of the chairs into the sun, using a towel for a pillow. Sunlight gleamed off the silver lenses of her glasses.

'She's a looker, eh, lad? What do you think?'

'Haven't met her.'

A DAY IN THE LIFE

'Always a cautious one, you are.' He brought his cane around and leaned his chin on the ferule. 'Know her number?'

'No.'

'Number Seven.'

'Your move.'

'Eh, lad. Oh, yes.'

The Admiral's face composed itself line by fold by jowl into an exaggerated concentration, and he placed a finger beside his nose, peering blearily down at the board. Then he reached out, lifted an ivory figure, and set it down on a white square, vulnerable and tempting.

Reply:

Pawn took pawn.

The old man smiled, moved a Knight in reply.

'Knight to Queen's Bishop three. You prefer, then, Admiral, the Scotch opening?'

The play went swiftly.

'What? Castling so soon?'

Somewhere, out of sight, a brash young band swung into a Beatles tune, *Michelle*.

Four moustached young men in gaudy silk uniform led the band. Behind them a group of men marched in Salvation Army grey. Their leader had the hangdog look of the existentialist intellectual, steel-rimmed glasses, a French horn, and a chartreuse suit with red piping. He was followed by a shifty-eyed, big nosed trombone player in pink with blue braid; a sweet-faced choirboy fingering an oboe; and last: a stern-faced lad in a scarlet tri-corn.

Down the beach the girl in the bathing suit had turned in her chair and lifted her glasses for a look.

She was beautiful.

And some mornings it was:
   'You there, Number Six, wake up.'
   The cool grey light of the television flickered against the living-room floor and its speaker rattled with sharp, insistent demands.
   'Get up, Number Six. I want to talk to you.'
   The bathroom tile was cold, the tap water icy and fresh.
   'You haven't been adjusting, co-operating. Why is that? Is there anything we can do to make your stay more comfortable? Is there something you lack?'
   But the shower was hot. Steam rolling up the walls in a pebbly grey finish.
   'We have tried to satisfy you, tried to help you fit in. Just what is your problem? We'll be glad to help, if only you'd ask. That's all we want, really, to make you happy here. What is it? What can we do? Answer me, Number Six. Do you hear? Speak up.'
   A small sauce pan, a large pat of butter, a quarter cup of flour, some salt, a pinch of cayenne, and milk.
   'Speak up. I will not tolerate this silence. It is your duty as a citizen to speak. I demand you answer me.'
   The yolks of four eggs beaten until thick (the shining metal blades cutting into the rich yellow vitelline).
   'Answer me. Speak up. I'm warning you. I won't tolerate this kind of disobedience. You can't flout authority in this manner. You can be made to speak, you know. There are ways of dealing with you.'
   Then the whites, whipped to stiff peaks.
   'Come in here where I can see you, this instant. I will brook no further delay. I want to see you and I want to see you now. I know you're in the kitchen. You're always

in the kitchen. You'll make some woman a wonderful wife someday. Your culinary expertise is well known. Now get in here and listen.'

Fresh, springy bits of cheddar dropped into the pan, and the flat plastic blade of the spatula stirring it in.

'There simply isn't room in this Village for someone who will not cooperate. We all have to work together to make it a fit place to live. And it will take all our efforts. The welfare of this Village must come before that of any one individual. Surely you see that?'

Then the yolk into the cheese batter and the mixture over the whites.

'We can only progress if we progress together. We must work in harmony and good fellowship. That's the only way we can build a community free from distrust, dissent, and unhappiness. One family, working together, playing together, living together. That's our ideal, a true mutuality of mankind. If you would seek to know what you could do for others, not what they might do for you, you would find rewards of which you have never dreamed.'

The whole into souffle dish and into the oven.

'Our differences of opinion need only be set aside to achieve mankind's dream: Community. There need be nothing to mar our brotherhood. And in this golden isle, all will shine more brightly.'

An hour of calisthenics and a fifteen-minute jog.

Then breakfast.

'I want to see you here, in my office, at four o'clock. Do you understand? Number Six, answer me! Four o'clock. Not a minute later. I can have you brought, you know. I don't have to be polite. You've been allowed more than enough freedom in the past. It's a privilege you've abused. If you can't accept its responsibilities—Was that the door? Did you—'

A DAY IN THE LIFE

The voice cut from speaker to speaker in the grey morning fog.

'I can see you, Number Six. I know what you're doing, where you're going. There are no secrets in this Village, no private existence. There is no need for privacy when all men are as one. Why not join us, give us a chance. We stand ready to help you. You have only to ask.'

The tall, candy-striped poles with their square metal hoods and glittering camera eyes waited at each corner, speakers crackling with cool electric life.

'We are simply not going to accommodate ourselves to you. Get that thought out of your head. You're not that important. You have a certain value to us, yes. But nothing so great as you think. You are no more than a cog in our machine, and you must be made to work smoothly. You will be made to work smoothly. There is room only for harmony. And we will *have harmony.'*

Number 105's house was shuttered and dark. The roses bright with dew.

'Think about that: harmony and beauty. A village living in peace and contentment, a model for the world to follow. Oh, if you'd only let yourself go, you'd find us the best of fellows. There's so much to do, you could really be quite comfortable here. It's only your attitude that can't be tolerated. We love the real you.'

Ting-a-ling-ling.

Chop. Number 87's cleaver cut through the beef. Chop. Chop. Chop. Steady, even slices, the silver wedge of the blade striking down against the wooden cutting board. Chop. Chop. Chop.

'Good morning, Number Eighty-seven.'

A mean, resentful look from tiny eyes set deep over quivering, sullen jowls. 'Number Six.'

'And how are you this morning?'

THE PRISONER

'Well enough, thank you. Your order?' He produced pad and pen.

'Chopped liver.'

'Off today.'

'In that case...Kippers, definitely kippers.'

'Off today.'

'What would you recommend?'

'Couldn't say.'

'One of those steaks...No. Not the fat one. That one there.'

'Some people...know-it-alls...' he muttered. 'Disparaging a man's...'

'What was that, Eighty-seven?'

His hands moved deftly, folding the meat tightly into paper. 'Here. That'll be point eight five credit units.'

'Charge—'

'All right.' He frowned down at the register. 'Getting quite a balance, you are.'

'Bill me at the end of the month, *as always*, and have this deliver—'

'No deliveries today.'

'No?'

'No. Number Twenty-four quit. Taken up a new career. Film-making it is. Just like these lads today: no sense of values. This profession was good enough for me father and it is good enough for me. Don't see why they have to go off and get themselves involved in that foolishness.' He picked up the cleaver and made an abrupt downward motion. Chop.

'Be seeing you.'

Chop. Chop. Chop.

Ting-a-ling-ling.

'*—in the Cultural Centre at two o'clock...And the Women's League for Better Government will hold a*

A DAY IN THE LIFE

benefit showing of Gone With the Wind *in the Little Theatre this evening at half past seven. I repeat: There will be a display of the sculpture of our own Number Three Thirty-six this afternoon at two in the Cultural Centre. And this evening at half past seven the Women's League for Better Government will hold a benefit showing of* Gone With the Wind. *It's for a good cause; please come and help promote mutuality in our Village. It is forty-two degrees centigrade and the wind is two point three miles an hour from the north-northeast. This is your Hostess, Number Two Fifteen, turning you over to the music of Mantovani with his arrangement of Yesterday.'*

The day was grey, heavily overcast, the underbellies of the clouds moving in dark, ragged streamers. The wind chill, a faint foretaste of rain in the air. Gravel popped underfoot and the white gingerbread houses stood out sharp and vivid, grey-gabled roofs like battlements raised against the sky.

Ting-a-ling-ling.

The man sitting behind the counter, bent over a rolling machine, was large and beefy, a thin reddish beard covering his cheeks. The shop was pungent with the aroma of tobacco.

'Yes. May I help you?'

'Where is One Fifty-seven?'

'He is no longer here.' The man did not look up from his work.

'What do you mean, "no longer here"?'

'He left.'

'For where?'

'I wasn't told.'

'People do not just leave this Village.'

'He did.'

THE PRISONER

'Why?'

'He was no longer wanted. He was not mutual.' The man lifted his massive head, eyes fierce and black. 'Why? Was he a *particular* friend of yours?'

'No. I merely came to inquire about my order.'

He pulled a ledger towards him. 'And you are?'

'Number Six.'

'Yes, of course,' he nodded. 'I might have known.' He pushed the ledger away. 'I'm afraid your order hasn't gone through yet.'

'What do you mean, "not gone through"?'

'All orders have to be initialled by Number Two, you know.'

'And he hasn't initialled it?'

'He could be busy. You know how these things are. I'm sure he'll get to it soon.'

'In the meanwhile, do you have any left?'

'A few.'

'Might I have them.'

'Yes. Of course.'

He brought out a box. 'There's one more. Do you want it now?'

'Will you hold it?'

'If you wish.'

'Please.'

'You're a polite one, you are.'

'Be seeing you.'

Ting-a-ling-ling.

On the opposite side of the green the young film makers were grouped around their camera, one of them panning it slowly across the Village. A woman stood next to the blond leader. She raised a hand in greeting. 'Yoohoo, Number Six. Come here a moment, won't you?'

A DAY IN THE LIFE

'Good day, Number Thirty-two. How are you this morning?'

She regarded him thoughtfully, brow dimpled faintly in a frown. 'There's something I want you to hear, Number Six.' She turned to her companion. 'Tell him about it, Five Sixty-nine.'

'Uh...' He scowled and fingered a calibrated lens hanging from his neck. 'It's like this.' He looked around warily. 'My mates say you're O.K. Thirty-two, well, she says you're a regular bloke, too. So I guess I should tell you. I hear you're in trouble, in dutch with the authorities, see. They wanta get you, you know?'

'Get me? How?'

'Oh, well.' He looked at the ground and then up towards the sky. 'I don't exactly know. I just hear it, that's all.'

'Where?'

'Oh, come on, man. Don't push me. That's all I know. Period.' He walked off towards the camera.

'Number Six?' Her eyes were troubled, worried.

'Yes?'

'Why do you persist? You can't defy them forever. My husband—poor Harry—he tried it, and look what it got him. Ah, don't you see,' her voice fell to a whisper. 'You could at least pretend to give in, like the rest of us.'

'I'll keep it in mind.'

'Hello, Number Six.' A boy with a large nose greeted him.

'Hello, Number Twenty-four.'

The boy looked worried, nervous.

The beach was cold, rank with a stench of ocean and seaweed.

'There will be a class in "The Village—Its Charter and Government", 7 A.M., Tuesday the nineteenth, in the Civic

THE PRISONER

Centre Meeting Hall. You're all urged to attend. Citizenship is your right and privilege. Exercise it. Become more mutual today.'

'Ah, lad,' the Admiral waved from his umbrella, 'a bit brisk today.'

'If you'd rather—'

'No. No. That's all right. A drop of wine to take the chill off and I'll be fine.'

A pawn was offered and rejected.

The new woman, Number Seven, came past them down the beach.

She was young, in her early twenties, with dark hair and a slender figure. She had a wistful expression, compounded of bitterness, disappointment and hope. And she looked at everything with a quick, uncertain glance, as if hoping in it she might find something of value, but knowing she would not.

Their eyes met for a moment, then she moved on, not quite smiling.

It was raining. He could hear the drumming of it against the roof. And, as simply as that, he was conscious.

He lay quietly for a while and listened to the rain. It was a good sound, clean and substantial: above suspicion. The weather was (save himself) the only thing he could trust.

He drew in a deep lungful of the sweet morning air and sat up, flesh contracting at the chill. He got out of bed, went into the grim, intestinal pink bathroom, rinsed his teeth and emptied his bladder. Then he stepped into the shower and turned the hot water handle all the way around.

The water smashed against him, icy cold, shrivelling his scrotum and sending a hot flush up his spine and neck into his face. He picked up the soap and began to lather.

The shower turned warm, then searing.

'Good morning.' The tinny shout of the television was louder even than the steaming crash of the water. *'A cheery good morning. It's seven-thirty here in the Village. Time for us all to be out of bed and about our business. We've all got to do our bit, you know. A job for everyone and everyone at his job.*

'Cloudy today, with a strong chance of showers, clearing late tonight or tomorrow. Be sure to wear your rubbers and carry your umbrellas. It will be wet.'

He turned off the water and got out, towelling himself dry and combing his hair.

Two eggs on to poach, a muffin in the toaster, and ham set sizzling. He melted a little butter, beat in a tablespoon of flour, a pinch of salt, some nutmeg and a

THE PRISONER

dash of pepper. Then he mixed it with a third cup of cream and stirred till it was thick. A capful of white wine and a palmful of Swiss cheese finished the sauce.

He buttered the muffins, set ham on each, an egg on the ham, poured the sauce over the egg, added green pepper and chives, and sat down to breakfast.

There was a blistered, discoloured spot on the moulding by his feet. Must be a leak somewhere. He glanced up—the enamel was unblemished. Either water was trickling in down a beam or there was faulty plumbing behind the wall. This wasn't a reasonable place for plumbing, though, and he'd gone over the rooftiles quite carefully this summer.

He dressed warmly in underwear, trousers, sweater and jacket, then laid his topcoat on the bed and turned to the mirror. He parted his hair high on the right side, sweeping it back straight at the temples.

His reflection stared back: brooding, enigmatic brow, straight nose, severe mouth, determined chin, fair Saxon complexion and wheat-straw hair looking stubborn and defiant.

Finished, he draped the overcoat across his arm and went into the living-room. He took the polished mahogany lid from his humidor and selected a handful of cigars, fitting them into a silver case and pocketing the case. There were less than a dozen left; he would have to see about his order. It might well have been filled by now. They had always gone out of their way to supply his individual brand before. Had, in fact, placed them here in anticipation of his arrival.

He had not (on that first day) been surprised to find them. Thoroughness (he had already surmised and was later to accept) was one of their characteristics and, however difficult the obtaining of these cigars must have been, they had not stinted, nor had he suspected any motive beyond thoroughness.

But now (replacing the lid) he wondered: Had so trivial an annoyance been prepared even then? Was everything, from the colour of the bathroom (so hideous he almost could not resist painting it) to the leak behind the wall (which he would, here at the beginning of winter with no chance of escape in sight, have to repair) a part of their plan? Did they hope, ultimately, to diminish him with minutiae, one grain at a time?

Quite deliberately he stilled his thoughts and gave himself up to the savouring of a cigar.

He opened the door and went out.

The rain had stopped and a cool golden light shone on the whitewashed buildings. Drops clung like crystal to tree limbs, sparkling in the sun. And in the fragile, translucent air even the distant, gabled skyline was clear and sharp.

Then a cloud rolled before the sun, plunging the Village into shadow.

Something scraped, struck metallically behind him. He turned. The long bony fingers of a branch stirred against his window. It would have to be pruned, of course, otherwise it might shatter the pane during a storm.

He moved down the moist, gravelled lane towards the green.

Number 105 was already out, stooping over the roses in a far corner of her lawn. A drab brown coat hung round her shoulders and flapped in the wind.

'*Guten Morgen,*' he said.

She did not turn or seem to hear.

The sea wind touched him, acrid and strong. He slipped his topcoat on and cinched it tightly, thrusting his hands in the pockets for warmth.

Number 237 emerged from a house, rod and reel in hand.

'Good morning, Number Two Thirty-seven.'

The man looked up, a frown wrinkling his brow, sun striking flame from the fish hooks in his hat. 'Oh, it's you, Number Six.'

'Going fishing?'

He grimaced, speaking slowly, reluctantly. 'Yes, with Number Eighty-seven. On the boats. Sort of a holiday.

THE PRISONER

Been planning it a long time. Damn rain. Special permission from Number Two himself. Not going to let the weather stop us. Must run, you know.' He set off down the road, not looking back.

Ting-a-ling-ling.

The new proprietor put down a pipe and stood up. 'Yes? It's Number...'

'Six.'

'Six. Yes, of course. Come about your order I imagine.'

'Has it come?'

'Part of it. Humm. Yes, part of it.'

That's never happened before.'

'No. I dare say it hasn't. Rather unusual I should think.'

'How many have come in?'

'Six dozen. Six dozen all together.'

'Have you reordered?'

'Yes; expect I'll hear something most any day now.'

'Could you send a dozen round my way this afternoon?'

'Can't say, Number Six. Really can't say. My assistant's quit. Gone into film-making.'

'Yours too?'

'Yes. I heard tell Number Eighty-seven's quit yesterday.'

'Curious. I'll come back myself. About a quarter to five.'

'Very good. Be seeing you.'

'Be seeing you.'

Ting-a-ling-ling.

It had grown darker, greyer outside, and a chill mist fell, descending on neck and brows. He turned up the collar of his coat and moved quickly across the green, soggy turf.

'Hey, lad, wait up.'

A DAY IN THE LIFE

He turned. The Admiral hurried towards him, brandishing his cane for emphasis.

'I had—'

'Expected to find me home, no doubt.' The old man stopped and caught his breath. 'Would have been too, but my charwoman didn't come. Had to go out myself. Weather like this is no good for a man my age. It's mortal cold, Number Six. And the cold hurts. My bones ache and I feel a touch of fever. Still up to a game of chess though. Nothing better. A warm fire, a drop of wine, and an afternoon with a pleasant companion. That's the ticket. Come on.'

'My place or yours? Mine is closer.'

'Mine. Mine, of course. Expecting a visitor.'

'Who?'

They started across the green and the mist condensed, became rain.

'Eh, lad? What's the matter? You're looking thoughtful again. Dangerous sign. I've marked it before. Bound to get you into trouble.'

His hand indicated the Village. 'What more trouble could there be?'

Don't say that lad.' The Admiral shuddered. 'Don't say it. You're bound to find out if you ask. I always have and I've never liked the answer.'

They let themselves into a small, brick cottage set towards the southern edge of the Village. A great fire roared in the hearth and he was warm almost before they had entered. Papers, glasses and ashtrays were scattered around the tables, desk and floor.

'Damn woman always comes Thursday. Why didn't she come today?'

'Didn't you call her?'

'No answer.'

Then he remembered. 'Isn't Number One Hundred five your charwoman?'

'Eh? Yes, yes she is. Why, lad? Have ye seen her?'

'This morning, pruning her roses. I called to her, but she didn't answer.'

'Maybe she's heard.'

'Heard what?'

The Admiral settled back and narrowed his eyes. 'Don't tell me, you really don't know?'

'Know what?'

'You're *persona non grata* these days. There's a new Number Two and he's put it out that you are no longer to receive special treatment. I think he let it be known that he didn't consider you exactly kosher, not mutual, you know. That anyone seen with you might be suspect too.'

'What about you?'

'Bosh. An old man like myself? No one pays any attention to me.'

'Thank you, Admiral,' he said.

'Ah...here. Set up the board, while I find the wine.'

They played for some half-hour in silence.

'You there, Number Six. We know you're there. We know everything about you.' The television across the room had come on, and a man's face took form. Though the background (a wall-sized bookcase and lamp) were in normal colour, the face had a bluish, almost purple cast, lips dark as dried blood. The man had close-cropped hair, a bullet shaped head, small feral features and a sharp smile.

'Not everything surely?'

'We've had enough of your boarding-school humour, too. Times have changed. We can no longer afford the freedom you enjoyed in the past. We've allowed you cer-

A DAY IN THE LIFE

tain privileges before. That's over now. You've got to get in line like the rest of us. The age of the individual is past. This is the age of the common man. There was room for your kind once. No more. We must all march together, the same step, the same direction, the same goals. This is the road to progress.'

'An excellent move, Admiral. I have rarely seen a rook used to such advantage.'

'Nothing to it, lad. Just a sharp eye and an orderly mind.'

'Number Six, answer me. This minute! I want to talk to you. In fact, I want to see you right now, in my office.'

'Might I have another glass of wine?'

'Certainly, Number Six. Allow me.'

'You too, Number Three Hundred seven. We've had our eye on you for quite some time. You had better mend your ways.'

'Number Three Hundred seven. Is that your number? I didn't know that.'

'Just call me "Admiral".'

'Of course.'

'The world has been tamed. There is no room left for rebels. We have a peaceful Village. Our citizens are content. I will not allow you to disrupt them. You're setting a bad example for our youth. They are becoming upset and uncertain. We cannot allow that. You must be stopped.'

'Excuse me a moment, lad.' The Admiral rose and went into the kitchen. He came out carrying a large pewter vase. He tilted the television set face down.

'What are you doing, Number Three Hundred seven? You can't shut me off—'

The Admiral poured the water from the vase into the

back of the set. There was a sharp glare of electricity and the voice went dead.

'We can expect a repair crew momentarily.'

'Right you are, lad. They won't leave you alone a minute in this damned place.'

The doorbell rang.

'Good after—' She caught herself and stared up at him through the darkened lenses of her glasses.

'Number Six,' the Admiral said, coming forward. 'And this is Number Seven. She's a newcomer.'

They made themselves comfortable.

'You surprise me, Admiral'

She lifted her sunglasses and looked at him thoughtfully. 'The Admiral's been good to me. I ran into him my first day here. I was upset.' She had fine, sharp features, clear youthful skin, and wistful, disappointed eyes.

'Eh? That's all right, lass. Think nothing of it. We were all put off a bit, our first day here.'

'Your television...have you dismantled it? I tried that with mine, but they came right away and repaired it. There's no way to shut it off.'

'A little butter to make it run smooth.'

'Yes.' She gave him a final, wondering glance and then replaced her glasses. 'It is rather Alice in Wonderlandish, Number Six.'

'You're an American?'

'Yes.'

'What's an—'

Outside they heard the high, piercing warble of a repair truck.

The door was flung open and four men came in: two of them wore blue uniforms and severe expressions; the other two wore rumpled green jumpsuits and carried rectangular metal repair kits.

A DAY IN THE LIFE

'Number Six?' said one of the men in blue.

The repairmen went to work on the set.

'You, mate. I'm talking to you.' He pointed a hairy finger.

'Yes.'

'Come with us.

'All right.' He turned to the girl. She tilted her head up to look at him. His reflection stared back from the lenses: a tall substantial looking man in a dark suit. 'Number Seven.'

'Number Six,' she replied.

'Thank you, Admiral. I enjoyed the game.'

'I'll see you later, lad.' The old man's eyes were apprehensive.

'Be seeing you.'

'Come on, mate.'

Number 2 looked up, frowning. 'Good afternoon, Number Six. I trust you were not inconvenienced.'

'Not at all.'

'Good. I'll take that as a sign of co-operation. I shall expect to see a great deal more of it from you, now that I am in office.' His eyes narrowed. 'You don't remember me, do you?'

Should he? or was this just one more slight-of-hand? Then, for a moment, he could almost (like a ghost image in the far recesses of his mind) remember this face, this voice, this precise tilt of head and gleam of demonic eye. Then, as he reached, it was gone, like mist, before daylight of reason.

'No.'

'I was—'

Number 4!

'—Number Four then.'

Yes. And for a moment the period stood out with utter clarity. There was a sense of water, the sea, a small boat, a quarter mile of dirt track, the use of his car...Realities he could almost, but not quite make come clear, but which, if he could penetrate their centre, would be his. Then the vision was gone, only a dim impression remaining like a hauntingly familiar scent.

'You weren't so highly placed then.'

'I am now. That is what concerns us. That and your intractable attitude. My predecessors have been too lenient with you. They sought to win your co-operation with kindness. I've had experience with your peculiar kind of mentality before. I know how to deal with it. You will co-operate or you will obey, but you will change. Have I made myself clear?'

'Quite.'

'But'—his voice was built for harshness; it could not easily make the transition to conciliation—'things could be made easier for you. You could be set free. If only—'

'I'd tell you why I resigned?'

'I don't like that attitude of yours, Number Six. And I intend to do something about it.' He looked back down at some papers. 'Dismissed.'

The rain fell heavier and heavier, whispering over the ground and drawing premature twilight across buildings and shrubs. Purple clouds boiled across the sky, running before the wind. Leaves whipped up about him and the rain stung his face.

He turned the collar of his coat up against his neck and went down the street to the tobacco shop. It was dark and shuttered, a CLOSED sign hanging in the window. He glanced at his watch: four thirty-five.

He walked down away from the shop and went home.

Number Seven was waiting on the steps.

May I come in?'

'Yes, of course.'

'I was curious. Exactly what *do* they do when they are displeased?'

'It depends.' He took her coat and put it in the closet, switched on the stereo.

'On what?'

'I don't know.'

'You don't seem to have come into any harm.'

'Not this time.'

They sat down.

'You have before?'

'On occasion.'

'What was it like?'

'Would you care for tea, a drink?'

'Not now, thank you.' She took off her glasses. 'In a while.'

'I started to ask you something earlier.'

'Yes...Number Six is it? I'm not very good with numbers.'

He smiled.

She laughed and crossed her legs. 'Yes, it is rather absurd, isn't it. I wasn't very good with names either. Just faces.'

'Number Six.'

'Of course. I always remember them when I hear them and think myself a fool for forgetting.'

'How—'

'How did I come here?' She raised her eyes and met his. 'I was going to ask you the same thing. You see, I haven't learned much, really. Nobody here will talk,

THE PRISONER

except the Admiral. I like him. He's the only person I've met here I feel I can trust.'

'I feel very much the same.'

'And I haven't been able to get in touch with the authorities—Number Two, I think he's called.'

'Yes.'

'And it's been rather hard, all in all. I tried to get out, of course, but that's almost impossible. There's no train or bus or car. And when you try to walk out, those...I don't know—they're like balloons, only I think they're alive—they stop you. And they're heavy.'

'Guardians.'

'Is that what they're called? How appropriate. Anyway, there doesn't seem to be any way out, not easily, and the natives won't tell me anything, and the Admiral's rather vague. I thought perhaps, well, you looked decisive. That's a rare quality anywhere. And I thought, Sandra, that's my real name, Sandra Champaign. Ridiculous isn't it? But it's the truth, I swear it. Sandra, I said to myself, maybe he doesn't know anything, and maybe he does, and maybe he's one of the ones responsible for your being here, and maybe he isn't, but you've got to talk to someone sometime and he looks worthwhile.'

'I see.'

'Who goes first? What's your name?'

'You might not believe it either. It's the British equivalent of John Smith.'

'Then perhaps we had better stick to numbers.'

'Perhaps we had, Number Seven.'

'I'll go first, if you like, but I'd like that cup of tea, now.'

I don't talk like this all the time,' she said when he'd brought in the service.

'I didn't imagine you did.'

'It's...I don't know, like giving up cigarettes. There's a tension, it crawls right up and gets inside you and fills you with a kind of evil energy. Do they have grass here, do you know?' She cocked her head and watched him with a half-amused curiosity.

'No I don't. How old are you?'

'Twenty-five.' There was something appealing and pathetic in her eyes. 'I saw some kids making a film around town. I imagine they'd know if anyone would.'

'Your reason for being here?'

'I don't know'—she leaned her head to one side and looked at him again—'if there is a reason for my being here. But what happened was this: I was hitching by plane from Los Angeles to New York. Dylan is giving a free concert at Woodstock.'

'Hitch-hiking by plane?'

'It's something I learned when I was married. My husband was a very successful insurance broker and so we were given a lot of credit cards. Anyway, one day he came home and said he couldn't stand it any more at the office, that the way we were living was sick and that we had to go out and find out more about life and ourselves. We used our cards and went around the country. We were with the Poor People's March in Washington when the troops came in and levelled their shacks. We used to sit outside in the evenings and look through the smog, rolling dope and talking. After a while, we split up. He just dropped out of sight, and since he wouldn't go back to work, there was no way they could collect their money. I was in Florida so I went to the airport and after a while this gay cat took me to his mansion in the Bahamas.' She shivered. 'I'm talking too much. I better drink some of this tea. Delicious. God, I'd like some grass. Got to come back down to reality. This place is too much.'

'You were in Los Angeles—'

'Yeah, and this spade cat, he came up and said I looked like I was going to New York to see Dylan and he had a plane and he'd like some company to keep him awake. He was loaded—a TV star, I think—and he was going there to give acid away. Just for the vibes, you know?'

He stared back at her.

'So I got in his plane, and we went up, and I began to get sleepy, and he said, relax, go to sleep, he'd wake me up after a while. I did and I woke up here.'

'Remarkable.'

'You don't believe me?'

'It's no less likely than my story.'

'Say.' She looked around. 'Your place is groovier than mine. I mean, I haven't got a stereo. And that's a good one.' Her eyes narrowed. 'Why is that?'

'I asked.'

'And they gave it to you.'

'Yes.'

'Why?'

'I don't know.'

'How did *you* get here, anyway?'

'I had a job, a job in...security.'

'You were a spy?'

'Something like that.'

She smiled wistfully. 'I've known rock stars and dope dealers, but never a spy.'

'I resigned.'

A DAY IN THE LIFE

'Why?'

'I'd rather not say.'

'I can see that.'

'It was my refusal that brought me here. It's a rather bizarre detention camp, as far as I can make out.'

'A detention camp?'

'For a certain kind of person. Men and women for whom their government has the highest regard, but who possess information which is thought too delicate to risk in the world at large.'

'But surely, not all of these people...'

'Not all of them. Some, as far as I have been able to determine, are what they seem.'

'And of course some aren't either, but are the watchers.'

'Apparently.'

'Then what am I doing here?'

'Exactly what I was wondering.'

Do you come here often at this hour?'
'Yes. Quite often.'
'It's beautiful, isn't it.'
'Yes, very.'

They stood, not quite touching, watching the steam rise from the ocean, a rose mist above bronze metallic waves. Dawn had turned the western sky ivory, and the morning breeze, chill and damp, blew up, tugging at their clothing. A few grey birds wheeled across the sky, levelled and shot past in a great beating of wings.

She turned to him. 'People here don't trust each other very much.'

He started to speak.

'Oh, I see the reasons. But...people can't live like that. It isn't good for them. They become hostile and remote, willing to do anything. Their lives and other people's lives become valueless and meaningless. I can see that it's even happening to you.'

A bird cried.

'You don't like that, do you? But it's true. You're like a boxer out of training—I knew a boxer once, lived with him in New Orleans. You're not fit. You're restless and uneasy, out of your element. Do you really think you could have retired?'

'Yes.'

'Some people *are* like that. They can relax as hard as they work. Not me, though. I wish I could.'

He shoved his hands into his pockets and stared down at her.

'I've got to get out of here, you know.' Her voice was sharper, desperate. 'This place is no good for me. No good for anyone.'

THE PRISONER

'What do you want?'

'Don't—'

'I'm sorry,' he said. 'I've heard all this many times before.'

'And yet, you don't look like one of them. I can tell a lot from a man's face. And you don't look like one of the sheep, either. I don't understand you or the Admiral. I would have thought either one of you would have escaped by now.'

'It's harder than it looks.'

'Is it? I thought it might be. But you do want to escape, don't you?'

'I will escape.'

'You sound so positive. When?'

'I don't know. When the right time comes.'

'And when will that be?'

He shrugged again.

'Hey, there! Number Six.'

They turned.

It was the blond, gangling Number Five Sixty-nine.

'Number Five Sixty-nine,' he said, 'Number Seven. Number Seven, Number Five Sixty-nine.'

'Hello, Number Seven.' He looked up. 'Number Two's really out to get you.'

'How flattering.'

'No, mate, I'm serious. Me sister, Number Seventy-three, she's 'is secretary, and she's heard. He give orders you was to be picked up and brought to trial.'

'On what charge?'

'Search me. But I do know this: Me and my mates, we been thinking. This being called Numbers, that's for the straights. Get me—the establishment. Names is where it's at. And we been watching you. You don't put up with much. You don't take no bull—pardon me, miss.'

A DAY IN THE LIFE

'You know where I can get some grass?' she said.

'Oh, wow, yeah, sure. See me later, we're growing some up just east of town.' He pulled out a handkerchief and wiped his face. 'Like I was saying, you don't put up with too much, and well...we dig that, get me? We think you're okay. If we can help you we will. But from now on, we're gonna be more like you. You know, independent.'

'Far out.' She smiled.

'Well...I gotta be on my way, Number Twenty-four wants to see me. In some kind of trouble, I think. A nice bloke, but careless. Good day.' He went back up the slope and walked away.

'You seem to be quite popular.'

'In demand, at any rate.'

'What are you going to do?'

'Have breakfast. Care to join me?'

'Oh yes. This looks interesting. What will they do to you, do you think?'

'I don't.'

They mounted the steps to the restaurant terrace and went in to the steamy warmth of the dining room. He drew out a chair.

The corners of her mouth quirked. 'Are all British men so polite?'

'I don't know.'

'You don't give a lot away, do you?'

Before he could answer, she was looking out the window.

Number One Twenty-seven appeared beside them, producing a pad from the pocket of her uniform and staring down at the table. Suddenly she turned and looked straight at him. 'Oh, Number Six. It's all right. Really it's all right. I forgive you. I do. I understand now. Can't we just be friends and forget it?'

THE PRISONER

'Yes. Yes, of course we can.' He smiled.

'Good.' She seemed satisfied. 'Now, your order?'

He lifted a brow. Number 7 bit her lip. 'Coffee? You do have coffee, don't you?'

'Oh, yes, Miss. Though we don't get so much of a demand for it.'

'Good. Coffee and a roll.'

'What kind of roll?'

'Any kind. It doesn't matter. Choose one yourself.'

'Anything else?'

'No.'

'And you, Number Six.'

'Steak and eggs.'

'I didn't know Englishmen ate steak and eggs.'

'I picked it up in America, Number Seven.'

'Aught to drink?'

'Tea, please.'

She went away.

'What was all that about?'

'One of the less creditable episodes of my life.'

'You'd rather not talk about it?'

'No.'

She turned and stared out a window. 'Look.' She pointed.

A group of women, mostly in their forties, were marching across the green, looking angry and carrying placards. At the distance it was impossible to read the legends.

Her eyes met his. 'You know, I don't understand this place. Look over there.'

A television camera stared at them from high on the far wall.

'They know where we are and what we are doing and what we are saying. Your place, my place, all the houses

A DAY IN THE LIFE

I've been in, and every street corner, all have cameras and speakers. And yet, they're looking for you, and they haven't come to get you. Why is that?'

Number 127 returned just then and they ate.

Afterwards they went up the street towards her house.

'It's incredible, really, to think that this place exists. In the outside world, you'd never imagine it, not in a million years. Oh, some crackpot type who really believes in a "they" might. The kind who get their kicks seeing vast conspiracies behind every setback and pigmentation of skin. The kind of guy who watches *The Fugitive* and *The Invaders* and *The F.B.I.* But no one else would really take such a place seriously. And yet, being here, it all seems so inevitable. Insane, but inevitable.'

'Yes, I had that impression myself.'

'I mean, they never leave you alone and they never make sense, but they control you completely, and you never asked to be controlled or to be part of their system, but here you are, and there's no way to resist or to escape. The Establishment's Establishment, in a way. Disneyland with J. Edgar Hoover at the helm.'

They rounded a corner and the mob of women was before them.

They stood gathered around the bookstore window in an angry snarl of conversation. One of the placards turned full on:

VILLAGERS FOR DECENT LITERATURE
BAN SMUT!!
PORTNOY'S COMPLAINT MUST GO!!

One of the women detached herself from the mass and came towards them.

THE PRISONER

It was Number 105, wearing her drab brown coat. Her face was pale and her eyes red-rimmed from crying.

'*Entschuldigen Sie, Nummer Sechs.* No—' she caught her breath. 'I will the English speak. I must, Number Six. I must speak with you.'

'I was just going,' Number 7 said.

'Is. Please. Is not necessary.' The old woman stopped and clasped her hands. 'Not necessary.'

'No, really.' She put on her glasses.

'Be seeing you,' he said.

'I hope so.' She pushed through the women and went into the bookstore.

'Oh, Number Six, I've wanted to talk with you for long.'

'I called out to you this morning.'

'And I didn't hear! How stupid. I'm so upset. Please, you seem like a kind man, a...modern man. I don't like to ask—'

'That's all right. Let's go this way. It's quieter.'

The sun came out from behind a cloud and suddenly the day was dazzling white.

'I don't know what to do, myself. I'm only a woman from the old country.'

'What country?'

'And these times, they're different. Things are not what they were in my youth. They say it is progress and change. Maybe so, I don't know these things. But the way I was raised was good enough for my *mutter* and *grossmutter* and it has been good enough for me. It's these children I don't understand. Do you?'

'In what way?'

'It's my daughter, Number Six. My *liebling*. She's...she's gone off and...She's...' The old woman began to cry.

'In trouble?'

A DAY IN THE LIFE

'*Ja.* Exactly so. She has gotten herself with child.'

'She has?'

'Yes. It's that awful Number Twenty-four. I told her not to hang around with him. Trash, that's what he is. Him and that bunch he hangs around with. They don't work, they don't go to school, they just hang around and think up trouble. The devil makes work for idle hands. Many's the time I've told her that. There's the devil in that boy, I said. If only she'd listened.'

They reached his walk.

'Won't you come in?'

'*Danke. Nein.* It wouldn't be right. But what am I going to do? You're a man of the world. You've seen much of life. Tell me. Am I wrong? Is this not so much of a sin anymore? What is happening?'

'Is he going to marry her?'

'Him? That good for nothing! Never. I'm sure of it. If he'd been any good, it would never have happened in the first place. Only, tell me, God, what am I going to do?'

'Have you consulted his parents?'

'No. Should I? Tell me what you think.'

He looked into her worn, peasant face. 'Number One Oh five, I think that's exactly what you should do.'

'*Danke. Danke,* Number Six.' She nodded to herself and went off down the lane.

He opened the door.

'Number Six?'

There were five of them standing just inside the door. They all wore uniforms. And they all carried guns.

'You are under arrest. Come with us.'

Two

Two

On what charge?'
'A complaint has been brought against you.'
'By whom?'
'By a party who considers himself aggrieved.'
'In what way?'
'It is not my place to know.'
'Whose place is it?'
'Those whose place it is to know such things.'
'And when will I be advised of the nature of this charge?'
'At the proper time.'
'And when will that be?'
'When it is deemed necessary.'
'And who will decide it is necessary?'
'The proper authorities.'
'Just who are these "proper authorities"?'
'Those who have been duly constituted.'
'And who constituted them?'
'The people.'
'Which people?'
'The people of this village. Now, you will come with me. There will be no further arguments.'

They went out into the rain.

Lack of mutuality...a capital offence...well, I mean...there's never been anything like it before.'

'Number Two's orders.'

'Well...' The desk sergeant scratched behind an ear. 'In that eventuality...yes.'

Their eyes met. The sergeant's lips were pursed in a faint, embarrassed smile. 'I'm sorry, Number Six. Don't mean to hold you up. But this is not our usual job of work. Not at all...quite different, indeed. Not like that lot over there.' He pointed across the room.

Number 24 sat on a bench next to a belligerent old gentleman. The old man had the clean, angry look of an IRA captain: bloodless lips, glittering eyes, taut skin. Number 24 had a large neb, wounded poet's eyes, an olive complexion, and an expression of bewildered suffering.

The old man caught the sergeant's gesture and glared, lip curling back in a sneer. 'Fists like matured hams,' he whispered, 'for beating defenceless boys like you.'

Number 24's eyes grew wide and fearful.

'Not like that lot at all,' the sergeant repeated. 'Just lurking about. More for their own good, really...' He brought his lips together and unbuttoned his jacket pocket, extracting a ball point pen. He lay the pen on the desk next to a ledger, opened the ledger to a half-filled page and began to write.

'Number...You are Number Six?'

'That is not my name.'

'My dear sir'—the sergeant assumed an expression of almost bovine patience—'I am aware that your name is not "Number Six". That is your *official* designation—as

THE PRISONER

I'm sure you know. The question is: Are you or are you not known as "Number Six"?'

He lifted a brow at the sergeant. 'The question is: What do *I* wish to be known as? My name is—'

'My good man!'

'And I am not your man.'

'Number Six!'

'And I am not "Number Six".'

'What would you have me call you?'

'By my name.'

'But that would be impossible. You can see that, can't you? Surely a sensible man like yourself can see that. So many men have the same name, but there is only one Number Six.'

'I've been told that before.'

'Then, what would you have me call you?'

'What are men in my position usually called?'

'But'—the sergeant's eyebrows rose in astonishment—'that would be most unmutual.'

'But truthful.'

'The truth can only be an embarrassment.'

'Not for me.'

'You're only making it harder on yourself, Number Six. Now—Number: Six. Charge: To be specified—'

'When will it be specified?'

The sergeant gave a patient, forbearing sigh. 'I am hardly the one to know.'

'Who is?'

'Now look here! I have my job and doubtless you have yours. Mine is to process people as speedily as possible. Nothing more. Now, may I get on with my work?'

'As you like.'

'Cell: Six.' He turned to a constable: 'Take Prisoner, The: A Day in the Life to cell six.'

A DAY IN THE LIFE

'No fingerprints?'

The sergeant produced a document. 'See. Here: your photo.'

'Photos can be changed.'

'So can fingerprints.'

'I should have known. But, tell me, how can you be certain of my identity?'

'They know everything. If they say you are "Number Six", you are.'

'And who are *they?*'

'The monitors.'

'What monitors?'

'Number Six, I have no time for nonsense. Take him away.'

'Be seeing you.'

He was taken to a cell. The door opened, he was let in.

Across the room (mounted above the tiny, barred window) was a television camera. Below the camera sat Number One Fifty-seven, the old tobacconist.

He lifted his head, eyes dark and reddened. *'Bonjour, Number Six,'* he said. 'I'm sorry I've gotten you into this.'

'And just what have you gotten me into?'

The rabbity little man looked down at his hands. 'I've been selling the marijuana.'

'Selling dope?'

'Oui. Just so. You understand?'

'No.'

'I brought it with me from my home. My father had smoked it'—he gave a little smile—'and his father before him. All our family and our town.'

'How did you come here?'

'On a boat.' He made a ducking motion.

'What brought you here?'

'An advertisement.'
'What kind of advertisement?'
'For a position.' He seemed genuinely bewildered.
'Don't you find this village a bit peculiar?'
'*Je ne comprend,* Number Six. These things are not of importance. It is important only that I brought these seeds'—his palms opened as if the seeds themselves lay within—'and that I planted them and that it was wrong.'

He sighed and his shoulders slumped. His hands came back to his sides. 'I do not understand, but it is wrong. They tell me it is wrong. All my life I have done it. It brings a man relaxation and peace. It is one of the good things in life. Why do they always take away the good things? They take away alcohol. And women. They take away tobacco and money. They even take away God. Why they do this, I do not know.' He looked up. 'Do you understand, Number Six?'

'No.'

'My father, my grandfather, even my priest. Could a thing be bad if a priest partook without harm? He was a very holy man—even the Bishop once spoke favourably of him. But they have arrested me for it. And here I am.'

'And why—'

'And you are here because it is believed you were one of my associates.'

'One of your associates?'

'So they think.' Number 157 lowered his eyes.

'Why do they believe that?'

He made that peculiar ducking motion again and held out his hands. 'It is my fault.'

'*Your fault?*'

'Number Twenty-four's also. But really it is mine.'

'What happened?'

'Long ago—before you came here—I lived in the house

that is now yours. I built a compartment to hide it behind the shower.' He sighed deeply. 'I thought no one would look there. I made a mess. I am really not very good at these things. The room had to be repainted. I went to the hardware but the paint was so expensive. I have never been a rich man, you see.' His spread fingers indicated poverty. 'Not at all in the old country. And after we settled here, my wife became ill.' He shrugged. 'I bought some paint. It was the cheapest they had. A clearance, I think.'

'Rohz?'

'Oui, Rohz. I painted it and then I had'—he spoke depreciatingly—'some trouble with my heart.' His hand moved up towards his chest. 'I was in the hospital, you see. While I was there, it was decided you should be given my cottage. I was to be moved to one larger.'

There was a crack of thunder outside.

Number 157 started, and looked about anxiously. 'I became agitated; I asked Number Twenty-four to move my crop for me. But he neglected it until you were here, and then it was too late. When they arrested me, they searched your house too, and it was there.'

'A very pretty story, Number One Fifty-seven—'

They turned.

On the wall above the door was a television screen. Number 2 glared down at them from it. Light gleamed on his high, bald forehead.

'—but hardly one to charm the court. I think the two of you had better come up with a better defence than that or we shall very soon be forced to forgo the pleasure of your company.'

'Forgo?'

'Don't be coy, Number Six. You understand me quite

well. *The penalty for frequenting a place where narcotics are kept is: Death.*'

'I am hardly surprised.'

'*I wonder if you'll be as smug when you face the firing squad?*'

He smiled without emotion.

'*But you'll be well treated until then. You're still a valuable commodity: no sense damaging the goods prematurely. And, since you're deprived of the pleasures of your own kitchen, let me offer you the hospitality of mine.*'

'Is that proper?'

'*In this case.*'

'The menu?'

'*Whatever you like.*'

'Thank you.' He had, after all, been certain.

'*You may order now.*'

'Shrimp cocktail, a green salad, welsh rarebit, red wine—not too sweet or dry—a sherbet for dessert.'

'*And you, Number One-Fifty-seven? What would you like?*'

'For me?' He was astonished. 'Nothing thank you. My stomach...' His hands spread. 'I could not eat.'

'*Perhaps later? No? You're certain? Very well. Good afternoon, gentlemen.*' And Number 2's image faded from the screen.

There was the sound of rain and a cool wet breeze came through the window.

He turned around.

Number 157 had sat down on a cot. 'Oh Number Six. They are going to shoot us.' He shook his head in distress. 'I just know they are going to shoot us.'

Do the defendants,' the judge said, leaning back in his chair and folding his arms, a stern figure in periwig and robes, 'wish to make any statement in their behalf?'

'*Excusez moi,* your honour.' Number 157 made the small ducking motion of his head. '*Je ne comprend*'—'

'Please use English in addressing this court.'

'*Je regrette*—' He shook his head. 'I'm sorry, your honour. I can speak English, yes. I am upset. I become confused...' He spread his hands in abjuration. 'I speak in French.'

'That's quite all right. Take your time. This court assures you a fair trial.'

'Well your honour'—he looked timidly up at the judge—'I want to say: This man, Number Six'—he pointed—'is innocent. He knows nothing. It was accident these things were at his house.'

'Excuse me.'

The judge turned his head. 'Yes, what is it, Number'—he hesitated—'Six?'

'Aren't these proceedings somewhat irregular?'

The judge assumed a kind of patriarchal indulgence. 'Number Six, I've heard a number of things about you. I won't say I believe them; I won't say I don't. But I will say this: You wouldn't have to ask me that question and you wouldn't be here today to ask it, if you had been more mutual in the past. The manner in which we conduct these affairs here is clearly set out in a course on the charter and government of this Village which the public was offered an opportunity to take last month.'

There had been such a course. He remembered the announcement distinctly.

THE PRISONER

'The procedure is quite simple,' said the judge. He lifted two stacks of IBM cards. 'These'—he hefted the one on the right—'contain all the information relevant to your case. These'—he indicated the second stack—'Number One Fifty-seven's. We will insert these, together with any facts you might care to present, into a computer. The computer will weigh the evidence and render an objective judgement.'

'What kind of "facts"?'

The judge smiled slightly. 'Just that. The factual evidence: fingerprints, photographs, tape recordings, film, chemical composition, the like. No biased testimony. No prejudiced witnesses. Just the truth. And an honest objective evaluation based on the facts.'

'But your honour,' Number 157 spoke up again. 'I tell you this man is innocent. He knows nothing.'

'He is not charged with knowledge. He is charged with "habituating a residence where narcotics are kept".'

'But your honour,' 157 said, 'this is not right. He knew nothing.'

'This law was enacted to punish participants at a narcotics party who were present but did not possess narcotics when arrested. It appears you are telling the truth. Number Two has even made an appeal in your behalf.'

'He has?'

'Yes, Number Six, he has. And very good of him too. But the law is specific, whatever its intentions: if marijuana was, indeed, stored in your home, however unwittingly, then you are guilty. If you are guilty, the penalty is death.'

The spray whipped back icy and sharp against him and he looked out over the bow of the boat at the building before them.

It rose up dark and square into the night, waves beating the cliff at its base. A dim phosphorescence clung to the rock, wet and gleaming.

The boat, caught between wind and ocean, tossed violently about.

He kept a firm grip on a stanchion and reached out to steady Number 157.

The little man looked up uncertainly. 'Where are they taking us, Number Six?'

There was nothing to say.

This building had certainly not been here a month ago, and yet he was sure that walls, floors, fixtures and cement, it would be authentic to the age of the smallest stone in the paving.

They were closer now, and heard clearly the crash of wave against rock. (Great foaming breakers smashed unyieldingly against the cliff.)

They slipped in along the base and entered a harbour. A guard stood on a dock and helped them make fast to the moorings.

Lightning flickered and there was the flat concussion of thunder. Rain poured down, blotting out sound and vision. A cold, miserable ache went along his back and a dull pressure started in his head. Suddenly the cold was piercing.

They were hustled off the boat and into a guard house. The room was hot and steamy, a dozen armed men swarming about. Number 157 turned to him. 'What is this place? I've never seen it before.'

'Neither have I.'

The room opened on to a lift. They were herded in. It began to rise.

'There are prisoners here, aren't there?' he asked.

'Yes,' one of the guards replied.

'Not by any chance an abbe?'

'No.'

'I thought not.'

The lift stopped and they went out on to a windswept courtyard and across to a door. There were steps in a chill corridor and they went down them carefully, one at a time.

The light seemed strange and his eyes ached.

They paused before a wooden door. Number 157 was thrown inward. The door closed, locked.

They went on. Another door opened. Hands closed on his arms. He was thrust inside.

He fell to his knees, in the deep pile of the carpet. A slender modern lamp lit the room. There was a red velvet divan at his elbow. He stood up dizzily and sneezed.

'Well, Number Six. It sounds as if you have a cold.' Number 2 grinned from the television.

An hour later his temperature was over a hundred and two.

Some days it was:
'Good morning, Number Six. And how are we today?'

He looked up at the starched white length of the nurse. Her face was lean, unblemished and plain. A stiff white cap sat on her hair. Her eyes were intense, almost maniacally cheerful.

'Did we sleep well last night?' She thrust a thermometer in his mouth before any reply was possible.

'We're certainly sulky today. Why is that?' She took his pulse. 'And our bowels—have we moved our bowels yet this morning?'

'Hello, mate.' The man on the next bed waved a red, freckled arm. 'What you here for?...Don't feel like talking, eh? I can understand that. Makes you miserable, don't it—the flu? I'm not really too sick, myself. But I figured, I got to do time, I might just as well do it as easy as I can. Of course, they aren't exactly stupid, get me. It ain't all that easy to put one over on them. But it can be done. I et soap myself. Made me sicker than a dog. I puked all over. Really something. Of course, I'm fine now, but they don't know that. Made 'em think I'm sicker than I was.'

'Breakfast, sir.'

Oatmeal, a poached egg, orange juice, two vitamin pills, one penicillin pill, one aspirin and two tablets he didn't recognise.

'Now me, I'm in for bombing a synagogue. Can you imagine that? For nothing more than trying to run those Jew bastards out of town. I say we don't need none of them in this Village. Hell, they use Christian babies in their services, don't they? Always lording it over everyone else, pretending to be so smart and so persecuted. I mean, they make their money off us, don't they? They exploit the working class, don't they? We gotta show 'em we're through with that, don't we?'

His lungs were dry and his lips were cracked with thirst. A fever burned behind his eyes and his face was hard as stone. There was no strength in his chest or arms; they seemed empty and bloodless.

'And how is the patient today?' The doctor took his pulse, glanced at a chart. 'Yes, yes. Very good. A touch of the flu. Nothing serious. You'll be right as rain in a day or so.' He looked at the chart again.

'Well...humm...uh-huh.' He left.

'Hello, Number Six.'

'Number Seven!' He was astonished. 'But—'

'How did I get here?' She grew thoughtful. 'I don't know. I heard you'd been arrested, and I asked them if I could see you. I didn't know you were sick too.'

'Yes.'

'What—' She looked around the sunlit infirmary. 'What are they going to do to you?'

'Kill me, they say.'

'Kill you? Do they do that?'

'Sometimes.'

'Do you—' She shook her head. 'It's hard to know what to say. Do you think they will?'

He looked into her eyes. 'I hope not.'

She smiled. 'I hope not either. But—' she shivered—'this place seems less and less real all the time. How do you stay sane?'

He was sorry the question was suspect. Suddenly he felt weak. 'It isn't easy.'

'I'm sorry. You look tired. I'd better go. Perhaps they'll let me come again.' She looked around at the room. 'Has this place always been here?'

A DAY IN THE LIFE

'I don't think so.'

'Amazing,' she said, and left.

They brought him lunch.

'I tell you, mate, it was a hell of a night. Them Hebes come running and screaming out of the place. Some of them was on fire and the women was mad to find their babies. And them kids, them kids were the best of all. They were crying for parents and some of 'em were so terrified they ran right back into the fire. Man, it was something to see.'

'A call for you, sir.' An orderly stood by his side, a plug-in phone in one hand. He fitted the cord into a plug.

'Hello? Number Six?' The voice was cool, young, vaguely familiar. 'It's Number Five Sixty-nine; remember me?'

'Yes.'

'I called your home and they transferred me here. Where exactly are you?'

'A prison of some sort. An island in the bay.'

'Yeah, I seen 'em putting it up. Funny, isn't it, them doing that? Well, we ain't gonna stand for it. We're all on your side.'

'How kind.'

'I mean, it's an unfair deal what you got, mate. You was innocent. Number Twenty-four told me all about it. This law's crazy, man. We tried to talk to someone. We tried to get through to Number Two. But nobody would give us the time. They said they was too busy. So we're gonna make your case known. We're gonna make people aware of this. If they won't listen to us when we ask polite, we'll force them to listen, get me?'

'I get you.'

'Well, I just wanted you to know. It's funny, in a way—them letting me talk to you.'

THE PRISONER

'I had that feeling myself.'
'Okay then, 'bye.'
'Goodbye.'
The receiver clicked off.

And some days it was:

'And then mate, we took the little vixen, well...she didn't go back to her German momma exactly the way she came. I mean, hell, it wasn't nothing to what the Jerries did to some of them Polack women. Why one time...'

The smoke from the man's cigar cut his lungs with a sharp, stabbing pain. Ceiling and walls boiled with colour. There was a dull pressure in his eyes and his ears rang dully.

'You, Number Six. We've come for you.' Two guards stood at the foot of the bed. 'Come on, get up.'

The words made a kind of dim, fevered sense. He could almost remember what they were. They had come to see him about something. Yes, they had definitely addressed him. He had heard them say, 'Number Six'. The words had roared distantly in his ears. 'Number Six,' they had said. 'We have come for you.' Now why had they done that? Thought moved reluctantly through his mind.

'The doctor says you're better today. We're moving you to a safe place.'

Moving? Today? He could not make sense of the words. His head was a blazing, flaming agony and he was only dimly aware of his body.

'Don't give me that. I ain't falling for it. They've tried that one before.'

The two men took him by the arms and lifted him from the bed to his feet.

'Come on. Get up. We ain't so dumb as you think.'

They let go of him and he collapsed.

'Ah, come on. Get up.' One of them kicked him in the side. He felt the blow dimly.

THE PRISONER

He was lifted again and carried out of the room. He never remembered anything more.

'*Good afternoon, Number Six.*' The television woke him and he came slowly to consciousness, eyes burning and dry, throat parched, lips cracked, tongue stale.

A group of men appeared on the screen. Soldiers in uniform, carrying rifles and surrounding:

Number 157, head down, stumbling forward, hands chained behind his back. A priest walked at his side, reading from a book.

The soldiers led him to a post, lashed him to it.

He was crying, face swollen with fear. He closed his eyes and bowed before the priest.

The priest touched a hand to his head, made the sign of the cross.

The soldiers put a blindfold over his eyes, stepped away.

The priest followed.

'*Ready!*' He heard the call faint but clear.

'*Aim!*'

There was a pause.

'*Fire!*'

The after silence was loud and sharp.

But today it was:
  '*FREE HIM NOW! NOW! NOW! FREE HIM NOW—*' The cry was deep and loud and threatening. '*FREE HIM NOW! NOW! NOW—*' It had the rhythmic inevitability of a freight train roaring past in the night. '*NOW! NOW! NOW—*' The faces of the protesters (young, long-haired, lank and angry) smouldered with resentment. '*NOW NOW NOW—*'

'*Your advocates, Number Six.*'

'Your rebels, Number Two.'

'*They are trying to save your life, after all.*'

'I'm flattered.'

'*It won't do you any good, you know.*'

'I hadn't expected it to.'

'*You're really a fortunate man you know. If you hadn't caught cold when you did, you'd be dead by now. This is probably the first time in your life you've ever been thankful for the flu.*'

'*NOW! NOW! NOW!*' They were on the steps of the Village Hall, fists raised to the blank grey windows. A line of guards stood before the doors, arms linked, faces bewildered and uncertain.

'And why,' an announcer's voice crackled from the speaker, 'are you doing this, Number Five Sixty-nine?'

'Cause it's unfair, man.' His thick blond hair stirred in the wind. He looked strong and righteous. 'Number Six didn't do anything. He didn't know anything about that dope. The courts proved that. It was left there by the guy who lived in the house before. Number Six is innocent. He should go free.'

'I see.' The newscaster was in his thirties and had

THE PRISONER

close-cropped hair. *'Well, why are you marching on the Village Hall?'*

'Because we've tried to talk to these people, with Number Two particularly. And they've refused to reconsider the case or even to speak to us.'

'And what do you plan to do if the police block the way?'

'Then we'll break through.'

'You're willing to use violence.'

'If they won't listen to anything else.'

'But isn't it true that Number Two himself made a personal plea for–' The sound cut off.

'An amusing situation, really. This young man thinks he can intimidate us.'

'What will you do?'

'That's right. You won't be around to see it. Will you, Number Six? That's too bad. I'm afraid we haven't made a decision yet. But we will and it will be an effective one. We have our ways, as you know.'

He said nothing.

'And yet, Number Six, you might still save yourself. You have only to co-operate and be set free.'

'No.'

'You're sure?'

'Quite sure.'

'Don't be too hasty. Is this secret more valuable than your life?'

'Apparently.'

'Then I wish you luck with it. Tomorrow is your execution.'

It seemed likely, then, that whatever they were going to try, they would try tonight.

He was standing before the window, looking out at the phosphorescent surge of the waves.
'Number Six.'

'Yes, Number Seven.' He had almost been expecting her.

She hesitated in the doorway, silvered lenses catching the light. 'You're not surprised?'

'To see you? No. You were too good to be true. Out of place, even here.'

Her mouth moved in a smile. 'Well, I'm close to true, you know.'

'Everyone always is.'

'The Colonel sent me.'

'The Colonel?'

'Colonel Schjeldahl, your superior.'

'My *former* superior.'

'Whatever, Number Six. I'm here to help you.'

'And how am I to take that?'

'Any way you want.' She took off the glasses and put them in the pocket of her coat. The Colonel wants you back. He has a project you may find tempting.'

'Is that the price of freedom?'

'Would you pay it if it were?'

'No.'

'He wants you to destroy the Village.'

'He does? Why?'

'Let him tell you.' She reached in her coat and produced a squat little gun. 'Here, I had to break in. There's a helicopter waiting on the roof.'

'From the Colonel?'

'Yes.'

'What about radar?'

THE PRISONER

'It's been taken care of. Our men are on staff tonight.'
'Our men?'
'Ask the Colonel, I haven't time to explain now.'
'Why is everyone always in a hurry just as things become most interesting?'
'Isn't life always the most interesting when the most is happening?'

They went slowly round a corner. He held the gun in a hand. A guard sat by a door.

The man looked up, the meaty pockets of his eyes creasing with apprehension.

'Be seeing you.' He squeezed the trigger. A jet of vapour hissed from the nozzle and shot up around the guard.

The man opened his mouth, straightened, and collapsed.

'It works.'

'Didn't you think it would?'

'Should I?'

'Think whatever you like, Number Six.'

He opened the door and they were out in the face of the wind.

The ocean was on one side, a stone wall on the other. Yellow light shone from windows above their heads and fell down against the flaggings. The night was black, and through it they saw the stationary lights of helicopter blades.

'*Your* men are on duty tonight?'

'It's a faction. Don't you understand, a faction. The Colonel's group is opposed to those who maintain this village. They have tried to have it phased out for years. But the men in charge have a great deal of influence. No one knows why. Maybe they like power.'

'What does he want me to do?'

'There are three directors. Collectively they are Number One. If they are removed the Village can be declassified and its prisoners released.'

'Removed?'

'Killed.'

THE PRISONER

'And where are we going?'

The cabin light came on and a man in a blue flight suit waved at them.

'To that unpronounceable place you chose to retire.'

'It's easy to pronounce.'

'Your car is at the hotel. We're to get in it and drive to London.'

They were almost at the helicopter. The pilot had switched on the engine and the blades were beginning to rotate.

'We're on Aran Island, you're sure of that?'

'Positive.'

'The north coast of Ireland?'

'Yes.' She brought out some keys. He took them. 'To your car.'

'Be seeing you,' he said, and shot her with the gas.

Three

He stood in the foggy Welsh morning and lifted his arm to look at his watch: the hands stood frozen at six.

The watch began to run.

The second hand swept forward and down. The works began to tick. He knew with a cold, sharp certainty that it actually was six: that their power extended even this far. He dropped the arm, lifted his shoulders to settle his jacket, and stepped forward on to the path.

Gravel crunched and popped underfoot as he went around the hotel to the drive.

He had glimpsed the emerald of his car from the air (moment's shock of recognition marring the landing as he brought the helicopter down, stirring up a fine wet lather from the golf course green). And now, as he moved through the misty, silent dawn its dew condensing on his face, he felt a terrible unease to know it stood there, defying logic in the chill reality of the day.

He turned the corner and saw it, shining and sharp, the long, clean lines of the *Flamberge* body, so much like the Rolls-Royce of MGs; the jaunty yellow hood, the green carriage, the polarised windscreen, the driver's door open and ready: engine running. He went round to the side and looked down at the interior. Yes, it was his, even to the scar of Janet's cigarette on the passenger seat, the tape in the player as he'd left it: *Surrealistic Pillow*.

The keys glittered, trembling with the low throb of the motor—gold chain hanging from them, his initials, J.D., on the fob. He reached in his trouser pocket: there was only the starched vacancy of the cloth at his fingertips. Yet those keys on that very chain had been there. He'd been given them as he climbed in. How, then, had they come here in the sun-filtered reality of the morning?

He looked across the sparkling lawn to the whitewashed façade of the hotel. It was silent and empty; nothing stirred behind the dark, shadowed windows. Yet he knew that this was the most popular resort in the Kingdom. And even it (as real and incontrovertible as the familiar tooling of the car here at his side) held a faint suggestion of unreality, like a set not yet in use.

Building (sharp and solid in the pearly light), air, shrubbery, worn stone fences: these were of the world he knew. Surely there was nothing sinister or harmful in them.

He turned his head and looked right, down the road. It wound up away from the grey-gabled houses of the village beyond. This much was familiar. This was real. This was the home he had chosen for his retirement.

'It's easy to pronounce,' he'd told the girl. And it was. Portmeirion, on the Pembroke coast of Wales, second home of Coward, Shaw, and Russell. As real as it was easy to pronounce. And, weirdly, less real—for this was the world he'd left: the mad Disneyland of the village.

Somewhere, a cock crowed, and he stepped into the car, settling back against the seat, and swinging the door shut. He closed a hand on the gear stick, shoved in on the clutch, and let the engine rev. It gave a deep, fullthroated roar, and he smiled, shifting into first and rolling forward over the drive and out on to the road.

The wind whipped in against him as he picked up speed, and he stared out through grey, polarised glass at green fields, hilly and rough.

The tarmac angled up, climbing the mountains, and he looked into the rear-view mirror, catching, for a moment, the reflection of the resort behind, its grey

A DAY IN THE LIFE

gabled spires the last visible reminder of the Village so far behind.

It dropped behind and was gone.

Then there was only the wind, the mist, and the roar of his exhausts in the primordial stillness of the dawn.

For, if he could not really trust this engine, at least he did not mistrust it. It felt right, as perfectly tuned as when he'd driven it last. This, then, was where he would let reality take hold: here, in this car, on this road, in this world he knew to be real.

Something in the harshness of the land, the strength of the rock, the preternatural silence of day, suggested a deeper, older, stronger reality than any they might alter or create. For the first time in two years, he let himself feel that there might be, outside himself, a place as secure and inviolate as that within.

The sun rose, a bloody disc behind the enshrouding fog, evaporating the dampness from his clothes, and the sleepy mutterings of birds, the bawings of sheep, the vague lowing of cattle woke to a clear, bright day.

He reached into a pocket and closed his fingers on a cigar, bringing it to his lips. He changed hands on the wheel, slid a hand into the other pocket and found the lighter.

The tart smoke filled his mouth. He let it out, changed hands again, propped his arm on the door, and relaxed.

There was much to decide, and his mind felt eager for it, ready and straining as if released from some ponderous weight. The question of reality (for all his determination) still plagued him, though he could no longer consider the green farmlands passing by a dream. The day (slender trees, blue sky, wind, car beneath him, the smooth grey surface of the paving) was too vivid, too real, too complete for illusion.

THE PRISONER

He rejected the possibility (not allowing himself to know that in illusion he might necessarily do the same).

He must, in any case, assume he saw a pattern behind their pattern, saw somewhere close to the truth. He had only one question: Where in reality would he find an answer to explain their madness? That he could predict them seemed a small enough victory if he could not understand them. He must see not only their design, but its source; otherwise he could at best counter them, never win.

He was, of course, even without that knowledge, still at an advantage. They could not control everything, he had to believe that. The reality of wind and storm, these (surely) could not be faked. They must count, ultimately, on his own self-betrayal: that he would become inundated by trivia and collapse from exhaustion.

Certain things were obvious. (A post stood at the corner of the road. Its faded iron sign read: SHREWSBURY, 38. He turned right with it and came down a levelling of the mountain into a valley.) The girl: she was fake, this much was easy to see. His escape was part of their plan. Only this present freedom was not faked: this was the real world, they could not be in control of it. He was free at last, and he must not miss his chance.

It was not so important that he remain free as that he reassure himself of the things freedom held. He must put his finger on the pulse of reality once and for all, that they might never shake him again.

He would have to see Janet, of course. She, at least, was the one thing on which he could depend. She and his mind. With so few weapons he would conquer.

He took a final puff of the cigar and flung it into the wind. The road dipped and the speed of the descent

A DAY IN THE LIFE

rushed through him, wind blowing back against his face, cooling the perspiration from his brow.

The miles swept by as the road rose and fell, curving past thatched-roofed houses, tall hedges and rocky fields, running south and east towards London.

He kept his foot on the accelerator until the last possible moment, then, just as he nosed down the ramp into the garage, he pressed in on the clutch, pulled back on the gear shift and then pressed forward: down-shifting. The engine roared sending high, whining echoes along the grey concrete walls and into the dimness below. Then the car levelled and he reduced speed, emerging on a vast level lot that shone harshly beneath a few fluorescent lights.

There were other cars around him, parked in neat, civil service rows, and he rolled forward, towards a gate. The gate guarded a steel-link cage. Before it, just to the side, and level with his right arm (as he pressed the clutch, the brake, and shifted into neutral, coming to a stop), was an orange box with a slot in front.

He took a hand from the wheel, bent towards the glove compartment and thumbed the latch. The card was there: on a pile of maps, exactly as he'd left it.

He picked up the card, leaned to the right and inserted it in the slot. As it went in, the interior lit and the box began to hum. When the card was fully inside it pressed back against his fingers and the light went out. The box clicked once and the gate began to rise.

He put the card back in the glove compartment, shut the panel, and settled back, shifting into first. The wheels bumped on to a steel platform caged on two sides with steel links: the front and rear were open. When he was just inside the gate dropped back, and as he braked to a

THE PRISONER

stop, the lift rattled and sank with a hiss of compressed air.

He felt a tense anticipation of the coming meeting and sensed that one more erosion in him. He was being immersed in an illusion so great it seemed to be reality itself. That was the core of their game: to create the illusion of illusion where only reality existed, and the illusion of reality where only illusion existed. For on the day he should readily fail to distinguish the two, their game would be won.

(An empty lot opened at his feet, rose, passed.)

He could not believe they had not seen that flaw: he had only to wait. So complex an illusion could not be maintained without error. And the moment they slipped he would know where reality lay. Proof lay on every hand (like substance within illusion) as solid and real as the chimes of Big Ben.

It was as if, in their determination to undo him, they sought not to ensnare him, but to subvert him. How else was he to explain it? Surely they saw the truth as easily as he.

(Another level, its Euclidean geometry vacant and empty, gaped, and closed.)

If they knew him, why did they labour so long against him when he gave them not even the satisfaction of his anger? Why was he thought a fit subject for their purpose? Unless it was in his very intractability that their desires lay: an awful perversion of reality in which their actions had no motives, their madness no object—destruction without reason.

He was finally (in the concrete reality of the lift, sinking below level after level of empty, shadowy lot) convinced he would defeat them.

A DAY IN THE LIFE

The platform moved past the interface between floors and he saw the flat, stained surface of the bottom lot.

The lift came even with the floor and stopped. Compressed air sighed, became silent. The metal gate lifted.

Something seemed to tug at the muscles of his neck. He turned his head: there was a camera mounted in the rear corner of the cage.

He looked down at the dash, shifted into first, pressed in on the accelerator and shot down the aisle towards a set of double doors in the far wall. He braked and swung left, switching off the engine.

He dropped the keys into his pocket, swung open the door, put a foot to the floor and stepped out. He strode directly to the metal doors, twisted his wrists out, seized the two handles, flung them wide behind him as he went forward into the room.

There was a square desk set in the middle of the floor: an intercom on its surface. A thin clerk with dark hair and dark eyes sat behind the table. There were four doors in the wall behind him.

The young man looked up. His chapped lips parted:
'Zed M Seventy-three!' he said in astonishment.
'I wish to see the Colonel.'
'Yes, Zed M Seventy-three. Right away.'

The young man pressed a button and spoke: 'Zed Em Seventy-three to see you, sir.'

The reply was low, tinny and indistinguishable.
'Go right in, sir. It's through—'
'I know the way.' He walked around the desk to the left hand door. It slid aside as he approached. He went down a panelled corridor and turned right. A plaque on the door read PRIVATE. He rapped perfunctorily and let himself in.

The Colonel (for just a moment he had a sensation of

THE PRISONER

utter wrongness) stood at the other end of the room adjusting the curtains on a night-time view of Piccadilly Circus and the jungle at its feet. The Colonel turned (and the feeling vanished beneath his need to know: how much truth was to be found here?), bushy hair and cotton-fluff eyebrows luminous in the shadow. His skin was smooth tan, liver-spotted, his eyes old and tired.

'Zed Em Seventy-three.' Eloquent brown eyes looked out from beneath tangled brows. 'I am pleased to see you.'

The old man limped up to him and stopped, gaze searching and intent. Then he sighed and turned his head, staring out at the metropolis below, 'Zed Em Seventy-three,' he said wearily, 'you are suspicious. That place'—the words were bitter—'has had its effect, even upon you.'

He followed the Colonel's gaze through the window to the smoky lights of the cars and the harsh neon of the marquees. And, with a numb start, like the beginning of fear, he remembered where he was, how far below ground. (The illusion had been so real he had not stopped to question, had had only that moment's unease for warning.)

The old man's head jerked around. He smiled. 'How do you like my toy?' He was proud. 'Never could abide these underground rooms. You remember? I asked to be moved upstairs from the beginning. But Housing refused, said they were hard put enough for space even with all these new excavations. So I demanded this.' His hand indicated the false window and he grinned. 'A television screen connected with a camera on the roof. It makes me feel less cooped up.'

Images (had they seemed like buildings, cars, streets only the instant before?) moved across the pane/screen:

flickers of light, suggestions of motion, darkness in irregular patterns. He seemed to be looking down the very centre of the maze to a place where, like an unanswered question, only blankness lay. Was this credible, or was it not? He could not escape the knowledge that, before the Village, he would not have paused to wonder.

'Interesting,' he said.

The Colonel's eyes grew thoughtful, sad. 'You've not come back as you went, that much is certain.' He shook his head and made his way to the opposite side of his desk. He drew out a high backed leather chair and sank down. 'Take a seat, Zed Em Seventy-three.'

'Thank you, sir.' He brought a plastic stool up to the desk.

The Colonel continued: 'They've changed you. You're tense and run down. You're no longer a healthy, thinking animal. You're apprehensive, nervous, suspicious.' The old man's eyes sought his and locked. 'Do you think you're up to killing?'

The question was like a knife-blade of reality, cutting at once—as if (and perhaps it was) deliberately planned—to the heart of his uncertainty: Would the murders be real or not?

'I think I am ready to do the job.' He was ultimately brought to so fine an equivocation as this.

'I'm glad to know that,' the Colonel said.

'I have some questions,' he said carefully. This was where he stepped fully into the unknown.

'I thought you might,' the Colonel answered.

'You sent for me?'

'Yes.'

'Then, it is a British installation?'

'The Village? Yes, it's ours, right enough.'

'And I was taken there because I refused to give the reason for my resignation?'

The Colonel nodded, sighed. 'Yes. You were so adamant that Sir Charles became suspicious.' The name sent a jolt down his spine, and the old man looked at him pityingly. 'Yes, Zed Em Seventy-three, your fiancée's father. He reasoned that if you were to defect, no matter what motive you might have, your veracity would prevent you from lying and that you'd refuse to answer altogether.'

'Perceptive of him.'

'Your loyalty was, after all, Sir Charles's responsibility.'

'And'—this seemed the worst treason of all—'Taggert went along with it?'

The Colonel's eyes were bitter, frustrated. 'He hardly had a choice.'

(That was true enough. It had been, after all, one of the reasons for his resignation.)

'You cannot imagine,' the Colonel said, and he felt a mortal dread, knowing what came next, 'how much easier it would be for all of us if you would just'—the old man's voice hardened—'explain your...retirement.'

'I think that best kept to myself,' he said, and felt restless at the limitation.

'I understand. This is no more than I expected. You see why I want the place destroyed.'

'Then,' he said abruptly, 'let's get on with it. Who are the men I'm to kill?'

He pulled in before the familiar red brick of his mews, shut off the engine, dropped the keys in his pocket, got out and went along the walk to the door.

(He tilted his head, staring through a chink between curtain and frame in the tall bay window: his front room was lit.)

The door closed and he went towards his apartment, body held tight in the expectancy of some further illusion.

The door swung open before him.

Beyond it the short, obsequious body of his butler stood framed in the light. The severe black of his suit curved round him like the carapace of a giant and sinister beetle. His face was swart, solemn, angelic (or stupid). There was something Montenegrin in the man's tiny smooth features, dark skin and bland expression.

He stalked into the room, wheeled (a warm 18th century landscape to his left, above the fireplace), staring down at the dwarf and frowning.

The little man stared back impassively, face a round rubbery mask, eyes flat and a little stupid.

'A Pernod, Sancho,' he ordered. He had, after all, a great deal to do. Tiredness was a hard ache between his shoulders.

The dwarf bowed, closed the door, and went past the bay window to the kitchen.

He let his hands fall and turned about, going over to the shelving.

The pale grey screen on the television was unlit, dustless, the blue wood shelves enclosing it dustless. He grasped the edges of the screen and pulled out: the front section of the chassis rolled towards him, swung to the side, revealed a wall safe in the back of the cabinet.

He knelt, reached in and twisted the dial to 0, turning it slightly to both sides, clearing it. Then he rotated the dial right to 21, left to 33, and then back to 12. The tumblers clicked. He let go and seized the handle, pulled down, then back.

The door came open. There were three stacks of twenty pound notes (four hundred pounds each) on the top shelf. A wide, flat box took up the bottom. He took a stack of notes and placed it in his inside coat pocket. Then he closed the door, raised the handle and spun the dial, locking it.

The dwarf was behind him, Pernod on a silver tray. He took it and sipped. It was almost disgustingly sweet: but the aftertaste—He shuddered.

A soft, muted chime rang at the door.

He looked up and nodded. The dwarf went to the door and opened it.

Janet.

She stood still, brown eyes staring, mouth (in the moment before surprise) precise, full, English. Her dark brown hair (cut tight around face and shoulders, as it had been when last he'd seen her) stirred him. Then she was moving towards him and he took her in his arms.

'John,' she said and pressed against him, too relieved even to kiss.

He held her tightly and, after a moment, said brutally: 'I can't tell you anything.'

She shivered and went tense.

'Isn't...Can you at least...' She hesitated, chose carefully. 'Is it a mission for my father?'

'No,' he said. 'I certainly can't tell you that.'

She straightened and pulled away, smoothing her dress.

A DAY IN THE LIFE

She looked up at him evenly, face strained and hurt in a way he had never seen before. 'I can't take much more of this.'

'Do you remember the message I sent you?' he said gently.

'John.' Her eyelids trembled in bewilderment. She seemed reluctant to speak. 'That was you, wasn't it? Tell me it was you.'

'Yes,' he said. 'It was.'

Her eyes, on his, were uncomprehending.

'There won't be much more,' he said. 'I promise you that.'

Her eyes were wide, the deep, luminous brown of the iris hesitant but hopeful. 'Is it over?' she asked.

'No,' he said, 'but it almost is.'

He stepped away and raised two fingers to the dwarf. 'Brandy.'

The little man inclined his head and went off.

Janet's hand reached out, seeking his: her eyes denied it, fixed on the cold brick hollow of the fireplace. He closed his fingers around hers (cool and strong to the touch) and moved towards the antique leather divan opposite the logs. Her eyes came around, puzzled, then understanding.

She settled herself back against the corner, face pale above the stark black of her dress. Mouth and chin were strong, severe, unyielding. There was something sullen and defiant in her expression: an unnatural gauntness in the cheeks.

'All right, darling,' she said. 'But it's a little hard to believe in a man for two years without seeing him.'

He went to the fireplace, knelt, and grasped the screen, shoving it aside so that he might reach the logs. He brought out his lighter, flipped back the top and snapped the wheel, watching the flame spring from the wick. He leaned forward and extended his arm until the lighter was under the shavings.

The flame licked out, singed the blond wood black, and a tiny nimbus of fire spilled up across the dry, splintered kindling. It blazed immediately, blue flame cooling upward to yellow. The fire seared the underbelly of the logs, popping and snapping.

'What's happening now,' he said, 'is so different from anything I have been through before that you cannot guess what it is like. Nor can I tell you. Yet it is, in its way, far more important than anything I have ever been involved in.' He leaned forward and looked straight into her eyes, seeking, by as much as it lay within his power, to insure her understanding: 'But you must understand this: I will not allow it to come between us or to hurt us any more.'

She looked at him for a moment, sighed and smiled with a deathly weariness. 'Yes, John.' She reached long, slender fingers to him.

He stepped forward and took them, the fine cool tension of her body (even if by so little) within his grasp. 'To tell you more would be to endanger you. And I won't do that.'

A tired, unhappy look came into her eyes. 'You are over protective, darling. Not knowing hurts more than anything that might be done to me.'

'Then I'm selfish,' he said abruptly. 'But I need your love too much to risk losing you.'

There was a sound of plastic on metal and footsteps coming across the carpet. The dwarf rolled the teacart up to them and stopped, uncorking the brandy and pouring equal amounts into snifters. The liquid fell and splashed, sparkling darkly.

A DAY IN THE LIFE

The little man recorked the bottle and bowed stiffly, then stood, waiting.

'Good night.' He dismissed the butler and seated himself by Janet, watching the dwarf go back to his quarters at the rear.

He closed thumbs and forefingers on the stems of the snifters and handed one to Janet, offering the other in toast. She took hers and sat back, watching him over the rim. Her eyes had a cautious, nervous intensity.

'To us.'

They drank the toast. Fire like velvet over his throat.

'How long will it be, this time?' Janet's face was tense, smooth, under control.

'How long...'

'Until you have to go back?'

He shook his head, 'I'm not going back. But there are a few things yet to be cleared up.'

'Are they—'She hesitated, visibly trying to come to grips with the question: eyes narrowing, mouth tightening. '—urgent?'

'Yes.'

She sat the snifter down and brought her gaze to his, catching her lip between her teeth. 'Then I must go. You see that: don't you?'

'Yes,' he said reluctantly, 'I see it.'

'Listen to me, John. There are only a few times in our lives when we are given the chance to love greatly. That kind of love is like a work of art. It's as difficult and demanding a creation as a painting or a symphony. You know that and I know that. We both know how magnificent its rewards can be. Now understand me. We have a chance at that kind of love, and if you think I shall let it be destroyed, you are mistaken. And if it comes to a

THE PRISONER

showdown between you and father—father be damned. I love you and I will have you.'

He waited.

'There is much I have to ask you,' she said. 'But it can wait. Will have to, I suppose.'

'Goodbye,' he said, and she was in his arms, crushed to him as his lips met hers.

They broke apart.

She smiled, touched his cheek, and was gone.

He knocked at the door: a sharp penetrating rap and the sound echoing away into the house.

A sheep bawed in the field behind and he caught its reflection in the great picture window just to the right of the walk. Then he heard the resonant silence of the wind as it rushed swift and cool across the earth. Down the road, near Kingsdown, a horn blared. All else was serene.

Something moved in the house. There was the muffled sound of a door closing. Then footsteps came towards the front.

The knob shook, rasped as if the other end were being turned. The door moved inward, opened the length of a chain. A short, white-haired man in a blue denim smock peered up at him.

'Yes?' the man said. 'What do you want?'

'Sir John Wilkinson, Bart?'

'Yes.' The repetition was shorter, harsher: impatient: 'What do you want?'

'I bear a message from Colonel Schjeldahl.'

The eye visible through the doorway grew brighter. 'Your identity badge?'

He slid a hand into the cool lining of his jacket pocket, fingers closing on the stiff plastic card, and brought it out, pushing it forward through the crack of the door.

Sir John took it (hands as smooth and pink as a child's) and lifted it to his face, peering at it carefully. Then he looked up, eyes bright and penetrating. He stepped back and closed the door; there was a scrape of metal on metal, and the door opened wide.

The hall was a sunny amber. An umbrella stand to one side of the door, a porcelain vase to the other. The pile

THE PRISONER

of the carpet was thick and deep, yielding easily to the foot.

He went into the living-room and turned to the baronet. Sir John offered him the card. He took it reading the familiar words as easily up-side down as right-side up: BY COMMISSION OF HER MAJESTY, THE QUEEN and pocketed it.

Sir John's face was kindly, softened by an amiable squint, flesh translucent and freckled. But there was something almost too companionable in its friendliness, as at the sharing of some off-colour Rotarian joke. Something too corrupt in his smile: the knowledge of some universal and unconfessed guilt.

There were gold leather divans along the wall facing the window, and antique writing tables at either end of the room. The whole had the faint decadence of eighteenth century Paris: gilt and lacquer.

Through the window he could see the damp countryside and the blue dome of sky. There was a rainbow over the road and the sun gleamed wetly in the grass.

Sir John gestured vaguely towards the divan. 'Make yourself comfortable.'

'I think we'd better have these shut,' he said abruptly, walking over to the drapes, shoving them aside, and closing his hand on the cord. He drew it down and the fabric swung out along the track, shutting off the view.

The old man gave him a sly, delighted grin. 'You know, I thought you were the one. I really thought I remembered your number.' He seemed to pause and consider. 'Yes, it was sent to me on a telegram. I've got it around here somewhere.' His head moved in little jerks, like a bird's movement, more excited than nervous.

'So it's finally come, has it? You know, I've always thought it would.' Sir John turned his head towards the divan. 'Is it all right if I sit down? I mean: is there enough time?'

'Sit down.'

'Good.' Sir John went over and sat down. He looked up, face relaxed, boyish. 'I've always speculated about what kind of person it would be. Just exactly what they'd be like. I wanted it to be someone, you know'—his eyes had a bright, far away look—'someone sensitive, intelligent, charming. Not a mindless, guttural assassin. Perhaps that's only vanity. Maybe I just want to think I was deserving of the best.' His eyes narrowed and he leaned back against the couch. 'If it's not asking too much: for which agency am I being *hit?* He seemed enormously pleased with the word.

'None.'

'But surely I am to be killed? I would hate to think my gesture had gone for nothing.'

'If I kill you,' he answered, 'it will be a personal matter between us.'

Sir John looked at him slyly. 'You know, that's very interesting. I had a conversation with Sir Charles Portland on that very subject.' He cocked his head. 'You do know Sir Charles, don't you?'

'Yes.'

'Good. Then you'll know Sir Charles is a very determined man. Well, I said that no one killed for purely personal reasons any more. That it was old-fashioned. That most men suffer so overwhelmingly from corporate guilt that they rationalise their guilt away by placing its responsibility on some larger object. That then they can commit any crime, on any scale, and be free of its consequences. Thus they can start at some relatively minute level, such as cheating on income tax, by deciding the bloody government takes too big a bite of their wages, and hang their guilt on the impersonal workings of the government.'

He paused and picked up a pair of wire framed glasses, settling them around ear and over his nose. 'Sir Charles, on the other hand, said that he knew of at least one person who did not suffer from collective guilt and who claimed he killed only from his conscience. Now in light of that, I find your arrival almost too opportune. Don't you?'

'It seems improbable.'

'But I had the distinct impression,' Sir John said, squinting upward and removing his glasses, 'that you wanted to question *me*. Is that right?'

'I have a few questions to ask.'

'Is that right? Will you use torture if I refuse to answer?'

'I hadn't considered it, no.'

'That's too bad. I've done a lot of thinking about pain and I've decided that, today, we are all too susceptible to pain. We are no longer conditioned to endure it. The surrender of our conscience has only been a symptom of an aversion to hardship. The public figures of our time condition us away from it. They endure nothing, are devoutly corrupt, and profit from their corruption. These are the people we seek to emulate—they fill the vacuum of our need for guidance.' He brought out a handkerchief and began to polish the lenses.

'People simply refuse to acknowledge evil in themselves or in others. It's a kind of societal blackmail in which everyone agrees to everyone else's equality. We expect and give no better than the other man—and we expect and give *nothing*. We never strain against opposition and our muscles atrophy. Ever wonder why so many American spies sign confessions when they're caught?'

'What do you know of the Village?' He had some time (after all) to ask the question.

'Which village?' The old man peered distrustfully through the lenses. 'The one just down the road? It's much like any other.'

'It's a place where a certain kind of person is sent. Persons who have held positions of some delicacy. Persons who are possessed of secrets vital to their governments. Persons whose freedom might represent a vital threat to their nation's security.'

'Do you by any chance mean a retirement village?'

'Persons who have been detained against their will.'

Sir John tilted his head to one side and peered at him from a single, intent eye. 'But surely, in these times, none of us are where we are entirely from choice. It seems clear to me that the forces of environment and heredity have channelled us down certain *inescapable* paths. What Negro in America is entirely free; what white in China is entirely safe? Aren't certain of your thoughts and attitudes a result of your upbringing? Too rigid and controlled a personality because of a strict father; a defiance and resentment of authority because of such fettering strictness.'

'I was thinking rather of deliberate, severe and brutal manipulation.'

'But are we not, in this world of ours, subjected to constant and inescapable manipulation? As subtle and persuasive as mother's instructions not to play with our penises, and advertisements that link smoking with sex appeal. As crude and overt as the public school's indoctrination of its pupils with Judeo-Christian morality, or the knowledge that if, alone, we indulge in certain pleasures, our entire society will punish us. And these pressures affect us in ways that are not entirely conscious; for the mind is not meant to be aware of its own defaults. Is not such manipulation, after all, common?' The old man gave a brief, questioning smile.

'How can you morally justify the existence of such a Village?'

'One can't, of course. But morality has become old-fashioned and without it anything can be justified. You see, when men begin to justify their actions in terms of something besides morality'—he hooked the earpiece to one lens around his ear, and paused—'their country, for instance, or their family, or their race, you can be pretty sure they've done something wicked. Since they are no longer acting morally, they do not wish to be reminded of morality, and if you talk of other things, they will not mention it.'

'And how do you, personally, feel about this?'

'Personally?' The glasses went on. 'We are no longer allowed personal scruples. If our government wages a dishonourable war, do we not have to serve? If our employers engage in shoddy practice, is it safe to protest? If our neighbours are offended, do they not threaten our lives? We are intimidated and circumscribed on all sides. We are forbidden personal feelings. There must be mass approval before we can act'

'And the people who are injured?'

'But isn't pain a universal of our lives? The pain of too loud a commercial, too long a queue, an unjust remark, a spiteful law, a loved one we cannot trust. Are these not the common experience of our age? And these people you speak of, who are they? Numbers, now, statistics, aggregates, masses, cogs in a system too vast to resist. How much do their individual lives differ—their problems, agonies, pressures and frustrations? Are they not the same in one village as another? Do men not carry their selves, their true problems, from one place to another as they move?'

'What about dignity?'

'Now? Dignity is dead. It went out with high button shoes and honest government. It was not compatible with computers and cost accounting. When a balanced book becomes more important than a human life, there is no room left for dignity.'

'You feel no responsibility towards these people?'

'Responsibility? We have been denied that privilege for some time in the search for a grosser national product. We have forsaken responsibility with guilt, and placed them both on the shoulders of something more nebulous than ourselves, something less accessible to punishment.'

'And'—he had to be absolutely sure—'you feel no responsibility for the lives you have ruined?'

The old man sighed and shook his head. 'There are no lives anymore, only statistics. Any statistic can be sacrificed.'

He reached into his coat pocket and closed his hand around the chill grip of the Colt. 'Even your own?'

Sir John Wilkinson lifted his head and looked up out of tired, cynical eyes. 'Even my own.'

'What it means,' the Field Marshal said, leaning forward on the frame and panting heavily, 'is fitness. We have to keep fit.'

His haunches lifted and his legs pumped furiously, as if this were indeed a bicycle and not a wheelless frame bolted to the floor. The steel bars on which he was mounted rattled with the pumping, and even the floor seemed to shake slightly.

'We have a duty, as a people and a nation, to keep fit. We cannot afford to be soft at a time when our enemies so completely surround us. It would be a flagrant invitation to conquest.' He stopped, panting heavily, and looked up. 'What newspaper did you say you were from?'

He got off the bicycle, took a few deep breaths, then lay down on the floor, pressing his hands flat by his chest and straightening his legs, rising on his toes. He began doing pushups, talking in measured breaths. 'Our enemies are ready. They will attack at the first sign of weakness. We must offer them the only thing they will understand: a solid, determined front. We must be strong, alert or they will destroy us.'

He stood and seized two handles set in the wall. There were weights connected to them. He shoved his right hand forward and a weight rose, 'What some people fail to realise is that, while freedom's the ideal goal, you can't have freedom without discipline.'

He let his right hand draw back to the wall and extended the left. 'I'm all for freedom, of course, but it does have its limits. Take a soldier at war: if he's allowed the freedom to talk out of turn, he may give his unit away and they'll be killed. Bet you don't think he should have it.' He let his left hand go back and began to raise

THE PRISONER

the weights, one at a time: a hard, dynamic rhythm—arms extending, then returning. 'And what about a clerk who knows a state secret—how much freedom should he have?'

He changed rhythm and shoved both handles forward simultaneously. His face became red and sweaty. 'It's the same with a civilian. Country's full of them. If they're soft, the country's soft. If it's soft the enemy will attack. A certain discipline must be maintained.' He let go of the weights. 'What newspaper did you say you were from?'

He took a rope down from a peg. 'Now I say: If the army can maintain discipline, the civilians can maintain discipline. After all, it's them we're fighting for.' He began to skip with an easy, loping stride. 'Now some people say the military's getting too big for its breeches. Well, that's a lot of loose talk. But a country is only as safe as it is strong. Any nation that thinks it can conquer it, will. Without strength, a country's lost.'

He coiled the rope and hung it back on the wall. 'In here.' He led the way into a smaller, padded room. There was a trampoline in the centre. 'You have to be able to defend yourself, or they won't leave you alone.' He climbed on to the trampoline and began to turn smooth, quick somersaults. 'Of course the enemy wants to undermine you any way he can. He'll try to get you with chemicals. And with slogans. And with fear. He'll pollute your water and corrupt your youth. If he's not stopped, he'll subvert the whole population. And do you know how he'll do that?'

'No, I don't.'

He got down off the trampoline and they went back in the gym. He worked his shoulders, flexing the heavy, slabbed muscles. 'What they'll do: They'll get people to

A DAY IN THE LIFE

be soft in the name of humanity. They'll lead people to believe that mankind is more important than survival. But a country has to be realistic.'

He scurried up the horizontal wooden slats lining walls and ceiling then grabbed hold of the overhead bars and crawled directly above.

'Sometimes, to save a country, a few of its citizens must be sacrificed. It would be foolish to risk national security because of one man.'

The Field Marshal bent his head, looking downward. 'Or don't you agree, Mr Drake?' then let go, falling, crashing down against him.

An elbow cracked his head and the room rang with darkness. He was slammed into the wall and air rushed from his lungs. Something sharp and wicked jammed into his back.

He was down on the ground with the other's body across his waist. The Field Marshal struck at his head. He dodged the fist and seized the arm, thrusting it sharply up behind the shoulder. There was concussion and he was asprawl the man's back, chin against spine, shoving up the hammerlock with all his strength.

They were rolling across the floor. He could almost see the face above him: it was hot and contorted, flesh bulging, whites of the eyes glistening.

Then he was on top, fingers deep in the other's throat.

He lay on the floor and a fist smashed into his face, splitting lip and cheek. He reached up and toppled the Field Marshal sideways, slamming his knee into the other's groin.

They were up against the pulleys. He was being held firmly back against the wall (fist clenched in his collar) and something hammered his face.

'Thought I didn't know who you were, eh?' The fist

struck him. 'Thought you had me fooled, huh?' And again. 'Knew who you were the minute I set eyes on you.' His right eye was dark. 'Heard about it the minute you escaped.' His lip seemed raw and burning. 'We all did. Even that old fool Wilkinson.' Again and again. 'It's not so easy as you thought, eh?' Again and again. The blows were powerful and stunning, almost painless, and in a moment he would be able to think.

'Been in condition every day of my life.' Again. (It was only a blur of motion and a distant sense of concussion like the foundations of reality being struck.) Again. 'Knew what you were out for. The girl talked.' AAGGAAIINN!! 'No need to call the guards. I'll take care of you myself.' AGAIN! 'Learn your lesson once and for all.' There was a dim, shattering red like the pounding of some cosmic pulse and a terrifying force tore through him. 'You're nothing special, after all.'

The mute appendage of his fingers clenched on a surface round and cool. His hand jerked upward against weight and there was a crack like a rifle shot.

The Field Marshal's head went sideways in a gout of blood. The drops flew out, gelatinous and warm.

His hand fell against the wall and closed on a slat. His muscles clenched and the chest was dragged upward. He came to his feet with the weight of the room at his back, skull empty and sore.

The Field Marshal had been knocked across the room and had risen to his knees, knuckles braced against the floor. 'Very clever. But hardly sufficient.' Blood ran down his cheek and his right eye was a raw, oozing mess.

He shook his head and threw himself at his opponent. They jammed against the bicycle frame and rolled into the room. He kicked free and sat up, bringing his hands together and clenching them into a fist. He turned quickly

A DAY IN THE LIFE

and smashed the other man in the neck. The impact jarred up the bone of his wrists and came together in his chest.

The Field Marshal fell back and kicked under the ribs, the pain like an axe blow to his heart. His lungs caught and he felt death in his throat.

The Field Marshal crawled over and drove shoulder into breastbone. His bones seared and turned to chalk. His left arm was grasped, and driven between metal sprockets.

He saw the Field Marshal's hand close on a pedal and shove forward. The chain bit into his palm and clamped down, the sprockets crushing through his hand.

Agony arced down his nerves and he heaved up, a single convulsive movement that knocked the old man loose and tore flesh from hand. He threw himself forward and caught the loops of the jump rope, jerking it down and over the man's head. He braced feet against body and drew sideways on the ropes. They tightened and gripped.

Good evening, Sir Charles.'
'Good Lord, Zed M Seventy-three, your face!'
He took a seat opposite the desk, and settled back, gun aimed at the older man's breast.

Sir Charles looked surprised, even concerned. 'What happened, man?'

'I had a fall,'

'Can I do anything?'

'Answer some questions.'

'I hope you realise the position you're in.' Sir Charles paused, allowing silence to underscore the words. 'There's no way in which you can escape. Security has been notified of your arrival and there are men outside every door. You were mad to come here.'

'I think not.'

'Surely'—Sir Charles's voice was incurious—'you don't think I'll let you kill me?'

'I'll kill you if I choose.'

'Would you care,' Sir Charles said, 'to tell me why you resigned?'

'I'm sorry, Sir Charles,' he answered. 'That will not be possible,'

'A pity. It's a decision you may someday come to regret.'

'Sir Charles'—there was really no other way to begin—'why this charade?'

'Zed M Seventy-three, I wish I could tell you.' Their eyes met, locked. 'But I'm afraid that, as you are reluctant to confide in us, we are reluctant to confide in you.'

'If you don't tell me, I'll kill you.'

There was the sound of a door opening behind him and a rush of footsteps.

THE PRISONER

Sir Charles leaped to his feet, kicking his chair out of the way.

Men closed in and one of them grabbed for the gun. He twisted sideways and fired. The bullet shattered Sir Charles's head and blew the skull against the wall.

'Jesus Christ, the bastard's killed him,' someone cried.

A fist slammed in against his already battered flesh, obliterating all consciousness. But as he was given up into darkness, he retained the memory of that shattered skull: the gleaming copper wires within the flesh.

Four

'Welcome back, Number Six.'

He stepped out of the helicopter and brushed off his jacket. 'Thank you, Number Five Sixty—' He noticed the badge. 'Sorry, Number *Two*.'

The youth grinned, half-pleasure, half-embarrassment, delight in his eyes. 'How do you like the promotion?'

'I thought the black leather jacket looked better unadorned.'

They went down the lane towards his house.

'You don't approve?'

'What difference does it make?'

'Well'—he scratched a leg—'I think a lot of you, of your opinion.'

'I don't like it then.'

'Why? I thought you'd be pleased.'

'Pleased?'

'Sure; you know.' He paused to wave at Number 87. The grocer waved back. 'I can do a lot in this position. It was me who helped you escape.'

'Really?'

'Say, don't you believe me?'

'Aren't you telling the truth?'

'Yeah.'

'Then I believe you,'

'I just wouldn't want you to get me wrong, Number Six. I like you. You got class. They offered to make me Number Two if I'd call off the demonstration. There were no strings attached. I can run things pretty much as I like. Of course I gotta go slow with the changes, cause there are these three old men gotta approve them, but I'm in charge. I had the alarms switched off the night you escaped. That proves I'm boss, don't it?'

THE PRISONER

They came up to the house.

'I had 'em in a corner, sir. We outnumbered them.'

'Well then, Number Two—' He turned at the door. 'What do you plan to do with me?'

The youth's brows creased in puzzlement. 'Do? I don't understand.'

'What am I to do?'

'About what?'

'Do I have to make myself clearer? Why have I been brought back here? If you're in charge, am I free to go?'

'Free to go, sir? Of course you're free to go.' The wave of his hand took in all the Village, suggested nothing more. 'Anywhere you like.'

'Outside the Village?'

'Why would you want to go there? Everything's all right here, now.'

Sometimes it was:
>Someone knocked at the door.
'Good afternoon, Admiral.'
'Damme, lad, I'm glad you're back.'
They shook hands.
'Well.' He settled himself on the couch. 'I didn't mean it that way. Only, I thought you might not be coming back at all.' He shot a look. 'You get me?'
'I've enjoyed our games.'
'Eh?' He brightened. 'So have I. So have I.' The old man paused and searched in his coat pocket. 'A mortal drop in honour of our friendship. What do you say?' He produced a slender greenish bottle.
'I'll find the glasses.'
The doorbell rang.
'How convenient. Come in, Number Seven.'
She leaned curiously forward and looked over his shoulder. 'Oh, it's the Admiral. Hello, Admiral. I'm coming in.'
He stepped inside and went in after her.
'Join us in a drop of wine, lass?'
'Thank you, Admiral.'
He got down three glasses.
'To Number Six.'
'To Number Seven,' he returned. And then: 'Your health, Admiral.'
'You know Number Twenty-four got married?' she said when they had all been seated.
'No, I didn't.'
'He got someone pregnant.'
'Would you care for tea?'
'Yes, please.'

THE PRISONER

'Admiral?'

'No thankee, lad I'll have a bit more wine.'

'Here, let me.'

He went into the kitchen and drew water into a pot. Number 7 came in behind.

'Number Six?'

'Yes.' He turned to face her.

'What happened?'

'In London?'

'Yes, of course.'

'Not much.'

'I'm not mad, you know. About being left behind. There was no real reason for you to trust me. I know what this place does.' She watched him.

'Not much happened,' he said.

'Did you kill those men?'

'Yes.'

'Then why are you back here?'

'There could be two explanations.' He put the leaves in the water.

'Which are?'

'One: Momentum. The order to return me was executed before they realised their leaders were dead. Two: It was a senseless attempt to confuse me.'

'Is that all you have to say?'

He poured through a strainer. 'What else is there?'

'There ought to be something more. You can't go out and do something like that and have it mean so little. What's the point, otherwise?'

'It did, though.' He handed her a cup. 'You'll have to accept that.'

'But I don't understand.' She followed him out.

'Neither do I.'

A DAY IN THE LIFE

'Eh? What's this? Secrets? Don't tell me. I don't want to know. There's too blessed many in this place now.'
'Then we shan't bother you.'
And they let it go at that.

And sometimes it was:
   'Yes, sir. May I help you?' The clerk came around the counter.
'I'd like a pane of glass.'
'What size?'
'Thirteen by ten.'
'Just a moment.' He went to a cupboard, returned.
'All out.'
'When will you have more?'
'Any day now. A shipment's past due.'
'Will you notify me when it comes?'
'Certainly.'
Ting-a-ling-ling.

The day was clear, brisk.

'Number Six.'

'Good afternoon, Number Two.'

'Where you off to?'

'The tobacco shop.'

He slung his jacket over one shoulder. 'I'm going that way. Mind if I join you?'

'Not at all.'

Their shoes crunched against the gravel.

'I thought you were going to do away with Numbers?'

'I proposed that, but there's been no answer. In fact, I haven't heard from Number One in several days.'

'Really? Is that usual?'

'I don't know. I haven't been on the job long enough to tell.'

'What do you propose?'

'To wait, I guess. I'm bound to be contacted soon.'

'Wouldn't care to send me off to investigate?'

'I don't think I'd better. I mean, I've got a position to maintain. A lot of people depend on me. I wouldn't want to disappoint them.'

'Well, I wish you luck.'

'Thanks, Number Six.'

Ting-a-ling-ling.

'Yes?' The bearded tobacconist stood in the shadows, face hard and recentful.

'I've an order in for some cigars. Number Six.'

'Yes. I remember. Well, they haven't come in. And I don't know when they will.'

'But number Two okayed them?'

'Yes. But nothing's come of it. Nothing's come in days.'

'Let me know if it does.'

THE PRISONER

'Be seeing you.'
'Be seeing you.'
Ting-a-ling-ling.

The breeze was warm and salty.
'What's that you're reading, Number Seven?'
'Portnoy's Complaint.' She held it up.
'Why?'
'I don't like censors.'
'Want lunch?'
'No.' She made a face. 'I've orders to avoid you as much as possible.'
'Why?'
'I don't know. Only that I must be careful not to be seen with you.' She tilted her head back and looked at him, then went off along the street.

But this time:
'*Attention! Attention please! This is an announcement of importance to everyone. Attention! Attention please! An important announcement:*

'*Citizens of the Village, this is Number Two. You are all to be set free. Those of you who wish to leave may do so. Liners will arrive next Wednesday to take you to Southampton. Passage to the destination of your choice will be provided there.*

'*Those who require a more extensive relocation may remain here until the details have been worked out.*

'*But you do not have to leave this Village. You may stay if you like. Repeat: You may stay if you like. We are not being closed down, merely opened.*'

It was good to be in London again.

He leaned back against the bus seat and looked down through the window at the street below. A newsboy stood in the grey twilight: a red and white sweatered figure against asphalt grey paving. The buildings were red, soot-blackened brick with dun, soot-blackened casements. There was debris—old newspaper, bits of cardboard, shattered plastic, a weatherstained playbill—blowing along the sidewalk and out into the street, where it was flattened beneath the wheels of passing cars.

MINISTRY SCANDAL—HIGH OFFICIALS SLAIN ROVING YOUTHS BATTLE POLICE IN PICCADILLY COMMUNIST PLOT CLAIMS M.P.

'So, you know, I says to her: If you don't get your arse into gear and go out and get yourself a job, I'm gonna kick your butt. And she says to me—get this: the girl's been laying around there ever since she got outta school, doing nothing but watching the telly and talking to boys on the phone—and where *they* get the time, I don't know—and I tell her to go out and get a job, and she looks up at me and smiles and says, "I don't know if I should, ma, I think I'm pregnant." And you wanta know something else: she says she don't know who the father is.'

'Well, I never. That's almost as bad as—'

KNIFING ON OMNIBUS
KILLER OF FOUR CAPTURED THROUGH ACCIDENT

There was a high-pitched scream.
'Leave me alone.'
A young man glared indignantly at his companion,

and as the bus came to a stop, he slapped the offender, leaped to his feet and stormed down the stairs.

The stench of sweat, wine and urine was unbearable. In the pastoral reality of the Village he had forgotten air could be so foul. The indulgent softness of the voices was like the sound of grease sputtering or the wetness of poured garbage. Their faces were coarse, hardened, impoverished, smouldering with resentment. He got up, went to the back exit and down around it to the street. A newspaper stand displayed its headline: OXFORD RIOT—65 ARRESTED.

A sign above the door read: FISH & CHIPS. He went in.

'What'll it be, love?'

'Fish and chips.'

'Aught to drink?'

'Ginger beer.'

She slid open the door of the fryer, reached in with a scoop. Two fat golden fish came out. She lay them on a paper and brought out the chips. Then she folded the paper into a neat parcel.

'Vinegar and salt?'

'Please.'

She got a bottle from the cooler. 'That'll be sixpence.'

He paid it and turned around.

A camera was mounted over the door, swivelling slowly from right to left. TELE-GUARD SECURITY CAMERA, the identification plate said. *Monitored twenty-four hours a day!*

He stepped out on to the street.

All motion froze. Reality ground to a halt. Everything was still, even (he was certain) the motion of particle and electron.

Some terrible dislocation wrenched through marrow and bone.

A DAY IN THE LIFE

Alone on the suddenly silent earth, he was as frozen as they.

This had been reality: deep in the fibre of his being, in the bedrock of his mind, he had believed this reality. Each blade of grass, each breath of air, each glimmer of light had seduced and compelled him. He had given himself up to the illusion.

And reality had broken.

Then, from far away, like the distant wail of the wind, a force blew up, stirring the dry grey dust of reality, and rising along his hackles in a frigid, blistering gale.

It lashed up about him and the fabric of reality quickened, grew thicker, took on life. The figures began to change. First their expressions (little flickerings of eye and mouth) and then their bodies (hair, complexion, length of limb, torso, stance and personality) began to change. They became farmers, businessmen, politicians, and peasants in a flickering blaze of change.

He saw every evocation of each visible personality throughout every incarnation down all history, all space, all time.

Light, sound, vibration, solidity and surface flared up in a great tumultuous cry. And the electric circuit of his nerves fused beneath too great an awareness as perception multiplied beyond limit and the universe closed in against him in a total, inchoate mingling of interior and exterior. All tissues, membranes, surfaces, interfaces and barriers vanished in a single gestalt instant. And transfixed by the experience of reality, he came finally to the centre of existence.

His mouth opened in a frozen, silent scream.

There was a moment which he became everything, and then—

Godhood.

THE PRISONER

His consciousness fled from the moment unable to accept, trembled and withdrew. It blanked out pain, blanked out cause, blanked out event, withdrew cell by cell, nerve by nerve through his every day in the Village to the time before that, to the source of the pain.

He fell, unopposed, to the day it all began.

The music pounded out of the speaker and the singer's voice set up an eerie summons, high and compelling. The shadows of overhead trees dappled and swirled off the car as it roared down the street and into the city rising before it.

His face was grim, set. Eyes, mouth, plane of the face, determined, stubborn and resolute. The singer's image was conjured in his mind, behind the brightness of the London afternoon.

The car rolled down a ramp into an underground garage.

He got out and went up to giant double doors, seized the handles and threw them open.

He threw the resignation on Sir Charles's desk.

Sir Charles looked up. His lips parted: The question was flung from the very depths of the universe itself:

WHY?

It smote his consciousness—all time, all structure, all reason ringing with the blow. Present and future mingled in his mind. Like the ghost of reality yet to be, he saw the Village more clearly than the face of the man before him.

And the memory of copper wire and jellied flesh was a shield within his hand.

'No!' he cried.

It was the ultimate affirmation.

The universe came to an end.

'*Veuillez*, Number Six, how did you resist?'

'Number Four was too co-operative, feeding me in prison. It was out of character. I ate and caught flu. Why? Obviously so I wouldn't be with you for the execution. Having found one illusion, I waited for the next. And after it, the next. There was never a time I believed completely in my environment.'

'*Merci*. At least I know.' He made a defenceless motion with his hands. 'What will happen to me now, I cannot say.'

'Perhaps you'll be given your old job back.'

'Yes, I rather like blending tobacco.'

'Well, if that's all—'

'Oh yes. You may go, Number Six.'

'Be seeing you, Number Two.'

He stepped out in the street and started home.

Number 237 was talking to a shopkeeper across the street. He turned and waved his hat. 'Hello, Number Six.'

'How was your fishing?'

'Good. Good. You must come to dinner and see.'

'I will.'

He went on across the green.

Number 32 came out of a store. Her skirt blew up about her legs.

Some days he would play chess with the Admiral.

And some days he would struggle merely to remain alive.

Today he had a window to repair.

And tomorrow...he would wait and see.

For he had defeated them, as he would always defeat them, learning more each time until he set himself free and left.

THE PRISONER

For one man alone, each victory against so great a machine must be sweet.
He lit a cigar and smiled.
Life was very good just then. Just then.

ALSO AVAILABLE

THE PRISONER
THE OFFICIAL COMPANION TO THE CLASSIC TV SERIES
by Robert Fairclough
ISBN: 0-7434-5256-9

It's been over 35 years since Patrick McGoohan's thriller series *The Prisoner,* a strange blend of espionage, psychodrama and fantasy, first entranced the British public. Every week, viewers watched as the eponymous prisoner, Number 6, imprisoned in a hi-tech Shangri-La-style village, was subjected to bizarre interrogation techniques and sinister scientific experiments. In turn, the Prisoner would try to escape his captors and, although always frustrated in his bids for freedom, he would sometimes be the moral victor by turning the tables on his anonymous persecutors. Tracing the program's evolution from sixties' curiosity to worldwide cult, the book examines the volatile social and political background which shaped its development.

With an episode-by-episode analysis, a wealth of previously unpublished photographs, production designs, props and memorabilia, production details, cast biographies and interviews with the cast and crew, *The Prisoner: The Official Companion to the Classic TV Series* is the ultimate guide to what is now viewed as one of the seminal television series of its time.

PACKAGED WITH A DVD CONTAINING A CLASSIC *PRISONER* EPISODE!

ALSO AVAILABLE

THE PRISONER
by Thomas Disch
ISBN: 0-7434-4504-X

He's a top-level agent, highly skilled and ultra-secret. But he wants out, and they won't let him quit. He quits anyway.

Then suddenly comes the dawn when he wakes up in captivity, in a pleasant, old-style, seaside town—one packed solid with electronic surveillance hardware.

This is The Village. And he is The Prisoner.

If he was good enough, sharp enough to be a top-flight cloak-and-dagger man, is he good enough to escape the men who've chained his life to the wall?

"Closely based on the extraordinary TV series, far and away the finest thing the medium has done in this genre; while Disch himself is one of the best SF writers."

—*Observer*